THE AWAKENING

BOOK ONE IN THE ZOMBIE UPRISING SERIES

M.A. ROBBINS

COTTAGE STREET PRESS

Copyright © 2018 by M.A. Robbins

All rights reserved.

No part of this book may be reproduced in any form or by any electronic or mechanical means, including information storage and retrieval systems, without written permission from the author, except for the use of brief quotations in a book review.

*For George Romero, the Father of the Modern Zombie Film.
Without his contributions, this book wouldn't have been written.*

1

The day the sun is blotted from the sky, and the winds of hell are upon us, is the day death takes possession of our land.

His late grandmother's words burst unbidden into Leo Nageak's mind as he opened the ATV's throttle and sped along the coastal tundra to Wainwright. Scorching wind buffeted his face, sending his shoulder-length hair whipping behind him. It was the fiercest heat he'd ever felt in his eighteen years on the tundra.

But it would have been worse if the sun were out. Overcast as hell, with roiling black and gray clouds, the weather had forced him to turn on his headlights. *Death takes possession of our land.*

Thirty minutes after he left Point Wallace, the headlights revealed a gaping hole in the earth and he pulled the ATV to a shuddering stop. The damn crater was big enough to swallow him and his four-wheeler whole. He hopped to the ground and removed his rifle from the ATV's gun scabbard. Peering around in the dim light, he scanned the horizon for any movement. An elder had encountered an aggressive young grizzly in the area a few days before, so Leo wasn't taking any chances.

Satisfied no danger lurked nearby, he walked to the edge of the hole and sighed. There were more appearing every day. The damn heat had been so bad, he wondered if the coast wouldn't melt into the sea. Even the elders said they'd never seen weather like it. According to his uncle's thermometer, it had hit ninety-five degrees the day before. Had to be a record.

Gazing out over the whitecaps in the Chukchi Sea, he considered his options. He didn't want to turn around, but what other choice did he have?

Maybe the ground isn't so bad inland.

He turned toward the shadow of Iqsigi Mountain in the east. He could ride up to its base, cut south, and still make it to Wainwright in decent time.

They called it a mountain, but it was nothing more than a big hill. He peered at it just as a small break appeared in the clouds. Iqsigi Mountain. His Inupiaq wasn't so good, but that's one word everyone knew. Of course, no one mentioned it if they didn't need to. If they did, they called it by its English name. Fear Mountain.

He wiped the sweat from his brow and hopped onto his four-wheeler. The elders had long taught that spirits lived in the mountain and would carry any intruders inside, never to be seen again.

"Bullshit."

Leo smiled that he'd said that out loud. As much as he might deny it, the damn stories still got to him. But a little tough talk would help keep his childhood fears at bay.

"Screw it."

He eased the throttle open and guided the ATV toward the mountain. The clouds closed in, plunging the area into a dusk-like darkness. Fat raindrops fell. Leo kept the speed low as the ATV bounced and bucked over the uneven ground, but the more inland he traveled, the smoother it became. He increased his speed.

The mountain grew larger, a big hulking shadow. He smacked his lips. His mouth had gone dry and he found it hard to swallow.

He'd swing by just in front of the mountain and be past it in twenty minutes. He increased speed again.

A flash of lightning shot across the sky, and thunder boomed, echoing through his bones. He gunned the throttle, and the ATV leapt. Rain poured down, and a lightning bolt spidered from the clouds, stabbing the mountain halfway up its slope.

Let me get through this. Let me get through this. Visions of spirits snatching him off his four-wheeler and dragging him into the mountain came unbidden.

Leo kept his attention on the glow from the headlights spread out in front of him. Tundra zipped by, with the occasional small bump shaking the lamp. Halfway past the mountain, the edge of a crater appeared out of nowhere. Leo released the throttle and jerked on the brakes. The ATV rattled and skidded. Hitting something solid, it stopped, but Leo kept going.

He flew through the air, weightless, then gravity kicked in and slammed him on his back to the ground, the impact knocking the wind from his lungs.

As he lay there, rain peppered his eyes and filled his open mouth, causing him to choke and struggle for breath. Then came the first jolt of pain. His back ached and his left calf burned, as if a hot poker were jammed in it. He coughed and cleared the water from his mouth. Taking a deep breath, he gagged at the thick smell of decay that assailed his nostrils. He turned his head and puked.

When he regained his breath, he looked around. Other than misty rain in the ATV lights shining above him, everything was blackness.

He moved his outstretched arms in the dark, and one hand landed on something cold and soft, almost like a fish's underbelly. He squeezed, and it made a disgusting squishy noise.

What the hell?

When he attempted to sit up, his left leg flared into agony. He fell back and panted.

No one knows I'm here. Gotta get up or I'll die.

He reached into his pants pocket and pulled his lighter out. The one his uncle had recently given him. He rubbed his thumb across the Marine Corps symbol on the outside, then flipped it open and rolled the wheel. Sparks flew and the wick lit, producing an orange-and-blue flame. Leo raised the lighter and his breath hitched.

He lay in a pit of frozen bodies, their mouths open in silent screams, arms outstretched, and legs in mid-stride. It was as if they'd been flash-frozen.

Or buried alive in the permafrost.

Leo cried out and sat up, the searing pain making him light-headed. He gritted his teeth and held the lighter over his left leg, examining it. A broken bone stuck out from the side of his calf, its splintered end red with gore. He swallowed. How the hell would he get out of there with a compound fracture?

But something about the bone's angle didn't look right. He moved the lighter's flame closer to the injury, then traced a finger gently down his shin, from the knee to the wound. Smooth. No break.

He gasped. The bone wasn't sticking out of his calf, it was sticking through his calf.

I'm impaled on a dead man's bone!

The lighter's flame blew out, plunging him into the graveyard's blackness. Leo groaned. He had to get free, but every movement brought a fresh wave of agony.

The rain stopped, but darkness remained. He wrapped his arms around himself, shivering. Sure, he was soaked from the rain and the pooled water in the pit, but how could he be so cold when sweat still poured down his face? Maybe he was in shock. If so, he was running out of time.

The wind died, leaving him with the putrid smell of thawing dead flesh. He tried breathing through his mouth, but that made it worse. Instead of just smelling the rot, the odor was so thick, it was like tasting it. Bile rose in Leo's throat and he choked it back. *Ignore it. Concentrate on getting out of here.*

He lit the lighter and held it closer to his wound. The calf didn't seem to be bleeding much, but that could change once he pulled it off the bone. He took his jackknife out of his pocket and cut his pant leg off. Not the best bandage, but it would have to do until he could get back to the village.

A scuffing sound came from the inky blackness beyond the lighter's weak glow. Leo's heart raced. His damn rifle was still with the four-wheeler. He raised the lighter and pointed the knife at the sound. Did spirits make sounds? Or was it the grizzly the elder had encountered, feeding on human carcasses? Either way, he was screwed.

Leo held his breath and tilted his head, listening. The sound didn't repeat, so he folded the knife and put it back in his pocket. He pulled his belt off. It'd be a serviceable tourniquet if he needed it, but he hoped that wouldn't be necessary. He had to catch a break at some point.

He peered over his shoulder. The edge of the grave, and his ATV, were a good ten feet away. From the way the four-wheeler's headlights shone over him, he figured he lay about three feet below ground level. The four-wheeler was still running, so it would likely be drivable. But how much fuel would it have left? Would he make it back, or die alone out there?

Don't think that way.

He steadied himself, his hands outstretched and propped on body parts. The damn things seemed to be thawing faster than when he'd first touched them. He pushed on the chest of a bearded man next to him, and it let out a belch. The stench gagged Leo and he turned away to keep his lunch from coming up again.

He waited for a minute, gathering his thoughts, then nodded. "Now or never."

Reaching out, he grasped just below his kneecap with one hand, and around the ankle with the other. *One, two, three.*

He pulled with his hands at the same time he pushed up with his leg. A wail welled from deep inside him, burning his throat and lungs with its intensity. His leg came halfway off the bone and stopped. Motes swam before his eyes and the world spun. *Stay awake. Please let me stay awake.*

Sobbing, Leo took great, heaving breaths and pulled again. The leg popped off the bone, but he didn't have the strength to ease it to the ground. Instead, it slammed down and all went black.

Leo's eyes popped open to a light show in the sky. Streaks of lightning crisscrossed above him, bathing the area in flashes of daylight.

How long had he been out?

His back throbbed and he struggled to sit up, a groan escaping his lips. Blood oozed from the gaping hole in his leg. Leo tried to bend it to get a closer view of the calf, but his leg remained motionless.

Shit. I can't even feel the damn thing.

Leo wrapped the pant leg around the wound. Even if he was protected from the pain, it didn't mean it wouldn't start bleeding the minute he moved. He scooted backward, then pulled his wounded leg after him. Gritting his teeth, he concentrated on getting to the edge of the pit. Scoot. Drag. Scoot. Drag.

A heavy crack came from somewhere in the darkness before him. *Shit.* Whatever it was, the damn thing was huge.

A crashing sound to the left. *And it's got company.*

Leo strained to go faster, his breath coming in great gasps. Tears poured down his face, but he didn't stop as he imagined a pair of grizzlies bearing down on him, just out of sight. What would it feel like to be torn in half by two of those monsters?

The crunching, shuffling pursuers sounded closer. Leo's arms burned with his frantic pace. *Where's the edge of this fucking pit?*

He backed into a wall of earth. Wasting no time, he grasped the edge and pulled himself up. When his legs were all that remained in the shadows of the pit, he had a sudden vision of the unseen predators grabbing his ankles and pulling him down to his death.

Grabbing his left pant leg, he swung his legs over and pulled himself to the ATV. Through pure upper body strength fueled by adrenaline, he muscled himself up with the handlebars. The gas indicator showed the tank to be half full. He whooped and swung his right leg over the seat, hauling himself to a sitting position.

He looked around to get his bearings. Behind him lay home. He'd have to go slow all the way back. If he got thrown again, he might never get back on.

A rustle. A growl. *That was no grizzly growl.*

A gnarled hand thrust to the sky and a pair of yellow eyes reflected the ATV's lights. Leo's breath hitched, then an ungodly shriek split the night.

Leo screamed, opened the throttle, and spun the ATV toward home.

2

The de Havilland Otter shook as it banked over the Chukchi Sea. Jen Reed checked her seatbelt for the tenth time, then glanced across the aisle at Devin. He sat with his eyes half shut, the turbulence not making any impression. If her old man wasn't scared, then she'd be damned if she'd show it.

He glanced at her. She tried looking cool as the plane bounced again, but her knuckles turned white as she clung to the armrest.

The pilot's voice came over the speakers. "Getting a little rough. Just stay strapped down and we'll be on the ground in a few minutes."

Jen tried to tighten her belt, but it was already as snug as could be. Devin turned to her, one bushy white eyebrow raised. "You OK?"

Jen shrugged, an unnatural gesture since her hands still clenched the armrests. "You've been through one landing, you've been through them all."

Devin leaned into the aisle and lowered his voice even

though there were no other passengers. "It's all right to be scared."

She turned toward him, a flash of annoyance heating her face. "I'm not afraid," she snapped.

Devin's expression didn't change, but he turned away and looked out the window. Jen could have kicked herself. One of the reasons she'd come on the assignment was to spend time with him. See if they could finally have a relationship. She pressed her lips together. She had to think more before she spoke, something she didn't have a lot of practice doing.

She peered out the rain-streaked window. They flew below the angry-looking black and gray clouds. Since it was July in northern Alaska, a time when the sun didn't set, she'd expected nothing but sunshine, but the weather patterns the past few years had been unusual. That, and there'd been historically high spikes in temperature. On the other hand, she wouldn't have been there if it weren't for the effects of the crazy weather.

The plane dropped a dozen feet, stabilizing with a slam that rattled the cabin. Jen waited for her stomach to catch up. She forced a smirk. "Next time I take a cab."

Devin made no reply. It was pretty obvious he wasn't used to her wisecracks. When not in the field, he'd spent his archaeology career in the stuffy halls of academia. It wouldn't surprise her that he'd never spent time around someone like her. But that's who she was, and he'd have to get used to it. Just like she'd have to get used to his lack of expression and periods of silence.

A village came into view, a cluster of houses huddled near the coast, with a large rectangular building in the middle and another on the inland edge of the town. A hill rose to the east, with a gravel runway on top and several large trailers on a flat area halfway up its slope. To the west was the sea and a smattering of boats.

The Otter swooped down, bucking and shuddering. Jen closed her eyes. *Let it be over.*

The plane bounced and swayed. Jen swallowed and let her head fall forward as if she'd dozed off. After several minutes she couldn't stand not knowing how close they were. She opened her eyes and did her best to fake a yawn just as the plane smoothed out, bounced once, and settled onto the runway. She was thrown against her seatbelt as the brakes squealed and the plane came to a stop ten yards short of the runway's end. *That's going to leave a bruise.*

The engines cut and the pilot came out of the cockpit, a smile painted on his face to complement a salt-and-pepper beard and mirror sunglasses. He opened the outside door. "Welcome to Point Wallace, Pearl of the Arctic. Watch your step while exiting."

Jen followed Devin down the short stairway to the ground. The wind had picked up and whistled across the hilltop, while the rain had eased into a steady drizzle. A slight break in the clouds offered a sliver of morning light. From where they stood, Jen couldn't see anything but the churning sea and endless tundra. She felt a pang of isolation.

A white crew cab pickup headed for them. It stopped, and a slender middle-aged man with receding gray hair stepped out from the driver's side.

Devin smiled and shook the man's hand. "Hal, good to see you."

He turned to Jen. "Jen, this is Dr. Parsons. Hal, this is my daughter, Jen."

Jen hesitated. Hearing Devin call her his daughter felt strange. But Dr. Parsons was the other reason she'd come on the trip. A chance for a young environmental scientist three years out of college to work with one of the legends of the field was an opportunity she couldn't pass up. She smiled and shook Parsons' hand. "It's an honor to meet you, Dr. Parsons. I wrote a term paper on your work on the effects of changing weather patterns on migratory animals."

Dr. Parsons chuckled. "Call me Hal." He raised an eyebrow. "I wasn't sure anyone had read that paper, so I'm honored. What have you been doing since you graduated?"

He wants me to call him by his first name? "I contract out doing fieldwork, mostly soil and water samples in remote areas."

Devin crossed his arms. "Contractor? I thought you worked for the state."

Jen shook her head. "I like to have control over my schedule."

Hal smiled. "We've only begun sampling, so we can certainly use your skills here. And I think we can expose you to some advanced analysis work, if you're willing."

"You bet."

The pilot carried their luggage over and placed it on the ground. "That should be all your baggage." He nodded at Hal. "I've got to get out of here, Doc. That cloud ceiling's coming down. National Weather Service says there's a hell of a storm coming in and aircraft will be grounded soon. I may be a crazy-ass bush pilot, but even I don't want to be up in this blow."

Hal clapped him on the back. "Have a safe trip back."

The pilot took two steps toward the plane and turned. "One other thing. There's a NOAA alert for increased sunspot activity. They expect moderate to severe communications interference for the next day."

"OK," Hal said. "We'll hunker down for now. See you in a few days."

The pilot saluted and strode off to the Otter as an older, rusted pickup rattled to a stop next to the plane. A thirty-something man with a trimmed beard and slick-backed hair climbed out and approached the pilot. Dressed in jeans and a flannel shirt with a big-ass gun strapped to his hip, the guy would've looked like a lumberjack if he weren't so thin.

"Who's that?" Devin asked.

Hal glanced at the man and frowned. "No one you want to know. He's our local bootlegger. Name's Griffin."

"Bootlegger?" Jen said. "He brews moonshine?"

"Point Wallace is a damp village. You can bring in alcohol for your own use, but can't sell it. Griffin brings in a lot more than one person can drink, but he always gets more."

Jen watched the pilot hand Griffin a box. Griffin laid it in his pickup bed and looked up, his gaze meeting hers. A half-smile broke out on his face. *Creepy.* Jen looked away.

Devin picked up his suitcase and reached for Jen's, but she grabbed it first. "I've got it," she said.

Devin hesitated, as if he were going to say something, but he stayed tight-lipped. He placed his bag in the truck bed and climbed into the front passenger seat without a word.

Jen frowned. She knew he wasn't capable of much emotion, but how could they establish a relationship if he didn't show it? *Or at least talk.* She tossed her suitcase next to his and took the back seat.

Griffin's starter chugged for a few seconds then started, and the engine roared to life. Black smoke belched out of the exhaust. Grinding the gears, he locked eyes with Jen and drove off, the truck disappearing over the hill's edge. A cloud of his exhaust whisked over Hal's truck. Jen wrinkled her nose at the stench.

Hal ignored it and started the crew cab pickup. He smiled at Devin. "It's been, what, twenty years?"

Devin grinned. Jen raised her eyebrows. Seemed he was capable of something more than a stone face after all.

"Twenty years," Devin said. "Ever since Gobekli Tepe in Turkey." He looked over his shoulder at Jen. "Hal was a medical doctor back then. Spent his time on archaeological digs, patching us up."

Hal shook his head. "I still can't believe I was able to fill my gravedigger position with the famous archaeologist, Devin Reed."

Jen squinted. "Gravedigger?"

"A term of endearment," Devin said. "The Chukchi Sea is eating away at the coast, and exposed an old native graveyard. I'm here to help the community relocate it to more stable ground. I don't usually work environmental studies, but I couldn't pass up time with an old friend."

Jen sighed. It took Devin talking to someone else for her to find out what the hell he was there for. When she'd asked him on the phone, he'd changed the conversation to the work he was doing then. She pressed her lips together. *This isn't going to be easy, but I'll make it work.*

Hal steered the truck down a dirt switchback road on the side of the hill. The village lay before them, sets of prefab houses patched with plywood and corrugated steel. Halfway down the hill sat three large white trailers outfitted with solar panels on a flat section of the slope. Hal pulled up in front of them and they all piled out of the truck.

Hal pointed to the middle trailer. "This is our headquarters and administrative offices. The trailer on the right holds our bunks and dining facility. You'll each be assigned a room." He nodded at the third trailer. "And this is a state-of-the-art lab. The best of its kind within the Arctic Circle."

Jen grinned. "Impressive. But do you have cable?"

Hal laughed. "A sense of humor, too? We'll get along just fine."

Devin pointed at a big gray tank that sat a hundred feet above them on the slope. "What's that? Water?"

"Fuel," Hal said. "We're mostly solar powered, but on days like today, we sometimes have to switch to generator."

He opened a door on the end of the headquarters trailer. "Come on. I'll give you the five-minute tour."

Devin and Jen followed him into a long, narrow corridor peppered with muddy shoe prints. Hal walked past a couple of rooms and led them into the third.

A cluttered room, it sported two desks and several bookcases stuffed with binders. The dense odor of old, burnt coffee hung in the air.

A thirty-something man with bleached blond hair and Clark Kent glasses sat behind one of the desks, hunched over a microphone while he moved dials on a radio panel. An older native man with a buzz cut stood in front of the desk, while a younger native man in jeans and a Grateful Dead T-shirt leaned against the wall next to him. He looked to be about Jen's age.

The radioman pressed a button on the microphone. "Wallace Science One to Wainwright Science One, do you copy?"

He released the microphone button, and loud static came from the speakers. The radioman adjusted another dial and repeated his request. He got the same answer.

The radioman shook his head. "Sorry. The solar activity is too great right now." He looked over at Devin and Jen and smiled. "You must be our new team members. I'm Pete Nance, Hal's assistant."

Devin nodded. "Devin and Jen Reed."

The older Native man offered his hand. "Raymond Kignak, and this is my nephew, Chris Nageak." Jen shook Raymond's hand, then stepped back so Devin could do the same. Raymond had a helluva strong grip for a guy who looked to be approaching seventy. She noted the Marine Corps tattoo on Raymond's forearm.

Chris nodded at Devin and Jen. "Good to meet you."

Hal cleared his throat. "What's going on?"

Raymond frowned. "Leo set out for Wainwright this morning. He was supposed to call when he arrived, but we haven't heard anything, and he should be there by now."

"None of our phones or radios in the village are working, but we thought yours might," Chris said.

Hal scratched his chin. "I wouldn't worry too much about it. He'll probably call as soon as the solar activity dies down." He shrugged. "After all, Leo was born and raised here. What kind of trouble would he likely get into between Point Wallace and Wainwright?"

3

Hal pointed to the last door in the headquarters hallway. "Here's the final stop on the tour. Devin, this is your workspace."

Jen's stomach growled. "How about we catch lunch after this?"

Devin glanced at his watch. "I agree. It's almost two."

Hal smiled. "Sorry. I get carried away sometimes with what we've done with the facility. We'll do a quick look in the archaeologist's office and head to the dining hall."

He opened the door and flipped the light switch. Florescent lights flickered on to reveal a twenty-foot-wide, ten-foot-deep windowless room with shelves lining the back wall. An autopsy table sat in the middle.

Hal moved to one of the neatly arranged cardboard boxes on one of the shelves. "You should have ample supplies." He pointed to labels beneath each box. "Body bags, surgical masks, gloves."

Devin pulled a box out and rummaged through the contents. "Damn fine setup considering how remote we are."

Jen's stomach growled again. "Unless you've got a

hamburger and fries in one of those boxes, I'd like to check out the cafeteria."

"Let's go then, shall we?" Hal said.

He led them out of the headquarters trailer just as Chris zoomed up on an ATV and hit the brakes. He skidded to a stop, sending gravel flying across the parking area. Cupping his hands to his mouth, he yelled over the engine, "Dr. Parsons, we need you right away at my uncle's house. Leo's back and he's in real bad shape."

Hal tossed his keys to Devin. "Start the truck. I'll get my bag and let Pete know what's going on." He ran into the trailer.

Chris sped off, spraying more gravel in his wake. Jen and Devin ran to the truck. She hopped in the back while Devin took the driver's seat. He pulled it up to the trailer just as Hal reappeared carrying a small satchel.

Hal jumped in and pointed to where Chris had disappeared over the lip of the hill. "Head there. The hill's slope is flatter from this point on, so it's a straight shot. Just take it easy."

Devin drove the truck over the lip and down toward the village. Jen rolled down her window, rain pelting her in the face, and took in the scene. The roads, nothing more than tire tracks between houses, were barely visible in the reduced light. They passed by a corrugated metal house with a dozen doghouses outside, a barking husky chained to each one. The truck's headlights picked up a handful of kids running after each other and weaving between buildings. They waved as the truck passed. Jen waved back.

Hal pointed to a large one-story building up ahead. The modern, flat-roofed structure stuck out like a sore thumb. It was as if someone had picked up a building from the city and dropped it in the middle of the village. "Turn right after the community center," Hal said. "Raymond's place will be the third house on the left."

Moments later, they pulled up in front of a larger house with an ATV parked outside. A pair of antlers hung above the front door, and a drenched American flag flapped on a short pole attached to the porch railing with duct tape.

Hal jumped out and ran into the house, leaving the front door open. Jen and Devin followed him inside just as the rain intensified and thunder rumbled overhead.

The front rooms consisted of a large, well-worn living room and a kitchen. The aroma of cooking meat filled the area. Jen couldn't identify the meal by its smell, but it made her mouth water and stomach grumble again.

Hal knelt next to a blanket-covered couch, talking to a young native man who writhed in pain, his eyes squeezed shut. Raymond stood at the head of the couch, arms crossed and worry lines creasing his face. Chris watched from the other end, his fists clenched by his side.

Jen stepped closer to get a better view of Leo. The man's clothes were soaked, and his left pant leg was crudely cut off and wrapped around his calf. Chest heaving with each raspy breath, his body spasmed, and something shiny fell from his pocket and bounced across the floor. Chris picked it up. He caught Jen watching him and showed her a worn lighter with the Marine Corps symbol embossed on the side. "Leo's lighter. My uncle gave it to him, and he'd hate to lose it."

Hal opened first one of Leo's eyes, then the other, and shined a light in them. Leo's pupils were so dilated, Jen couldn't see any part of the irises. Hal pursed his lips and untied the crude wrapping around Leo's calf. It dropped away and he gasped. Jen craned her neck to see. It looked like someone had drilled a half-inch hole through Leo's leg. The edges of the wound had turned black. Even with all that, there was only a little blood oozing. Hal turned away and coughed. A foul odor slapped Jen in the face. "Shit." She buried her nose in the crook of her arm and fought back the urge to puke. Devin made a disgusted noise next to her.

Hal looked up at Raymond. "Can we get some hot water?"

Raymond turned toward the kitchen, and an ancient native woman in a traditional kuspuk, a tunic-length hooded overshirt, shuffled out of the hallway. She looked a hundred if she looked a day. She said something to Raymond in Inupiaq, and he answered in kind. She nodded, limped into the kitchen, and took a glass pitcher out of the cupboard.

Hal pulled a stethoscope out of his bag and listened to Leo's chest. He shook his head and pulled out a blood pressure cuff. Leo jerked his arm away as Hal attempted to wrap it around his bicep.

With effort, Raymond held Leo's arm still. Hal wrapped the cuff and took the reading. He sat back on his haunches. "This is bad."

Raymond released Leo, who seemed to have settled down. "What is it?"

"His heart rate's increasing and his blood pressure's going through the roof."

"Islig," Leo moaned.

Jen furrowed her brow. "What'd he say?"

"Islig," Raymond said, his eyes on his sick nephew. "We call it a mountain, but it's more like a big hill. It's forbidden to go there."

Chris let out a loud breath. "Islig means fear. Fear Mountain. Where the spirits live."

Raymond leaned over Leo. "What about Islig? Were you there?"

Leo squirmed. "Bodies. Dozens. Hundreds. Death is in me. It calls to me."

A crash came from the kitchen. The old lady froze, her eyes wide. The pitcher lay broken at her feet. Lips trembling, she said, "Tuqunaragri."

Leo murmured something Jen couldn't make out. She leaned in closer. Raymond had bent down, and Hal cocked an ear. "What was that, Leo?"

Leo's eyes flew open, his irises huge and deep yellow. "It's in me!"

Jen stumbled back, stepping on Devin's foot, but he didn't seem to notice. His eyes were fixed on Leo, who kicked out and nearly connected with Chris's jaw.

Hal broke the spell first and fished around in his bag. "Hold him. I'll give him something to calm him down."

Raymond held Leo's shoulders while Chris and Devin restrained his legs. Leo's creepy eyes focused on Jen. Hair stood up on the back of her neck. What the hell had happened to the guy? She'd never heard of anyone with yellow irises before.

Hal injected something into Leo's arm. Within a minute, he relaxed and his eyes closed.

"He should sleep awhile." Hal listened to Leo's chest. "Better. Not great, but better."

Jen hugged herself. "What's wrong with him? And what the hell's up with his eyes? I'm going to have nightmares for months."

Removing a blood collection syringe from his bag, Hal shook his head. "I don't know yet. Whatever it is, it's moving fast, and he could lose the leg. We need to get him to a hospital."

Chris stared at the floor with his hands shoved in his pockets. "We can take him overland."

Hal frowned. "Normally, I'd agree. But his illness is too big of an unknown. He may not survive the trip."

"Maybe that bush pilot would go up in an emergency," Jen said.

Hal stuck the needle into Leo's arm. Dark red blood flowed into the collection tube. "He won't take the chance. Bush pilots are a bit crazy, but they're not suicidal."

"We've got to do something," Raymond said.

Packing away his equipment and the blood samples, Hal nodded. "I'll get these to the lab and see what I can find out."

Jen placed her hands on her hips. "We should go to the mountain and find out what happened there."

Hal stood. "No. We don't know what the hell's out there. It could be contagious."

Devin crossed his arms. "I'm with Jen."

Jen's eyebrows shot up. *He's agreeing with me?*

Devin continued. "If it's contagious, we already have it, so I'm going. I've been on several digs with biological hazards and can handle it. Time for me to be useful around here."

Chris stepped next to Devin. "I'm going, too. I know the way."

Jen straightened. "I came out here for a unique experience. If hunting corpses by a haunted mountain in the middle of nowhere doesn't check that off my bucket list, nothing will."

Hal's lips pressed tightly together, but he remained silent.

Jen strode to the door. "Time to find out what happened to Leo."

4

Jen stepped onto the porch. "So how do we get there?"

Devin turned to Chris. "We'll need equipment from the archaeologist's office. If we load it into the truck, will it make it out to the mountain?"

Chris shook his head. "Not a chance. You need a four-wheeler. I've got a buddy with an ATV trailer that'll hitch up to the back of mine. Unless you've got a ton of stuff, that should work."

Jen crossed her arms. "We're going to get real cozy if all of us ride your ATV together. Are there any others?"

Chris jogged down the steps and mounted his four-wheeler. "There are three more sitting in back of the head-quarters trailer." He started the engine and raised his voice. "Keys are hanging on the wall of the admin office. Meet you there." He waved and rode off, disappearing behind a house.

"What's your plan, Gravedigger?" Jen asked.

Devin scratched his chin. "Chris and I will go see what's out there. If there are bodies, my job here may have gotten bigger."

Heat rose in Jen's face. "What do you mean you and Chris? You're not leaving me behind. I'm damn sure not taking another step in that house, and I won't sit around a stuffy science trailer on my ass. I'm going, too."

"We don't know what we'll run into out there. Besides, the tundra's no place for a city kid."

"City kid?" Jen glared at him. "You don't know me. That's the damn problem. If you'd brought your ass around a little more when I was growing up, you'd know I've spent a lot of time in the wilderness camping, hunting, and fishing. I know how to ride ATVs and snow machines, how to make shelters and snow caves, and where to find food and water."

Devin's face fell. Jen clamped her mouth shut. She had lost control and overdone it. Again. That was how she'd lost her last three boyfriends. The rain picked up and Jen wished it would just wash her away.

"OK," Devin said. "You're coming. Let's get moving."

Jen stammered. "I-I'm sorry. I didn't mean to—"

"It's all right. I should've remembered what you told Hal about spending a lot of time in the field." He gave her a grin. "And you're twenty-five. Far from a kid."

Jen opened her mouth to thank him, but Hal rushed out of the house and they piled into the truck. Jen sat in the back, wheels turning in her head. She'd expected Devin to be combative and too set in his ways to change, but he'd shown her different. Was there hope for them to establish a relationship after all the time they'd been estranged? While he certainly wouldn't be a 1950s' TV dad, maybe there was room for mutual respect.

"What's the story with Raymond and his nephews?" Devin asked. "They seem extremely close."

Hal kept his eyes on the rutted road. "Their father left the village when they were still toddlers and never returned.

Their mother, Raymond's sister, died in an ATV accident when they were in their early teens. Raymond raised them as his own."

Hal parked in front of the lab trailer and stared out the windshield. "Look, I don't agree with what you're doing, but I can't stop you." He got out of the truck. "Just be careful." Without another word, he disappeared into the trailer.

Jen shrugged. "Isn't he Mr. Happy?"

"I'll go get the equipment," Devin said. "Can you get the ATVs?"

Jen hopped out of the truck. "Can do."

A peal of thunder boomed nearby as she hurried into the admin trailer. Still hunched over the radio in the office, Pete put a hand up as she walked in, then keyed his mic. "Wallace Science One to Barrow Control. Come in, please." He sat back and a garbled voice came over the speaker, but Jen couldn't make it out.

Pete wiped his hand down his face. "How's Leo?"

"Not good, but Hal's working on him." Jen scanned the wall. "Where are the ATV keys?"

Pete raised an eyebrow.

Jen sighed. "Hal knows. It's OK."

Pete hitched a thumb over his shoulder. "Next to Hal's desk. The gas tanks should be full, but check them just in case. Don't want to come up empty out there. Especially not in this weather."

"Do you have a couple of ponchos we can borrow?"

"Sure," Pete said. "That closet next to the file cabinet."

Jen grabbed the ponchos and two sets of keys and stepped into the hallway. She almost ran into Devin. She held the keys up and jingled them. "I'll check out the four-wheelers and pull them around."

He nodded. "I'll get the supplies and meet you out front."

Ten minutes later, Jen parked the second four-wheeler as Chris pulled up.

"How much stuff does your father have?" Chris asked.

Jen shrugged. "No idea. I've never been on one of the Great Corpse Hunter's safaris."

Chris grunted and went inside. He and Devin loaded the trailer on the back of Chris's four-wheeler.

Jen nodded at the ATV trailer. "There's still plenty of room on that thing."

"We'll need it," Devin said. "I plan to bring one of the bodies back for examination."

Jen and Devin started their ATVs. Chris cupped his hands around his mouth. "Stay close enough behind me to see my lights."

He took off down the hill. They followed him as he threaded his way through the village and out onto the tundra. The rain had slowed, and the thunder and lightning had stopped. A couple of miles out of town, Chris slowed to a halt and waved the others forward.

When they caught up with him, he pointed ahead. "See that ground there?"

Jen looked out where Chris's headlights shined. About ten feet ahead, the ground was pitted, and beyond that there appeared to be several large holes. "The heat is melting the permafrost," she said, "and the ground's collapsing."

"Would Leo have gone this way along the coast?" Devin asked.

Chris nodded. "This is where he would've turned toward the mountain."

Jen peered out into the tundra. A large shadow rose in the distance. "So what are we waiting for?"

Chris smiled and gave her a thumbs up, then gunned his

throttle and headed toward Fear Mountain. Jen hesitated long enough to make sure Devin was coming, then she followed Chris, ignoring the queasy feeling in her gut.

5

They reached the base of the mountain without incident and turned right, their headlights exposing the tundra as they rode along. A few minutes later, Chris slowed and gestured for them to stop. "We need to take it easy here," he yelled over the engines. "Leo's been riding this tundra all his life, and something caught him off guard. Stay behind me."

Jen and Devin nodded, then followed Chris as he eased the throttle open. They drove at a slow speed for another hundred yards, their headlight beams sweeping the ground, before the tundra ended and blackness lay beyond.

They stopped and turned off their engines, but kept their headlights on. "What the hell is it?" Jen asked.

Chris hopped off his four-wheeler and shook his head. He picked up a flashlight from the trailer and shone it back and forth on the edge of the darkness. "It's a big pit. Looks like the tundra caved in here."

Devin opened a large box on the trailer. "Help me with these."

Jen and Chris joined him, and he pulled out a pair of

cordless twin halogen lights on tripods. Jen and Chris both took one, and Devin grabbed another from the box. "I'll set mine up straight in front of the ATVs. Jen, plant yours twenty feet to my right, and Chris, plant yours twenty feet to my left."

Chris and Jen nodded, and Devin walked straight toward the pit. "Don't get too close to the edge, since we don't know how stable it is."

Jen set up her tripod a few feet back and waited for the others. When they'd finished, Devin pointed to the back of his light. "The switch is on the bar between the lights. Let's get these on."

Jen flipped the switch, and the halogens flooded the pit in bright light. Devin's and Chris's also came on. Jen peered into the pit and her heart skipped a beat.

The pit wasn't deep, maybe four feet, but was filled with hundreds of bodies. It reminded her of pictures she'd seen of mass graves, except the bodies weren't just lying there. They seemed to have been flash-frozen in the middle of some action, their arms askew and their legs ready to take a next step. She focused on a body just in front of her. Dressed in what looked like old-fashioned clothes, it had a chunk of its neck missing as if something had taken a bite out of it.

Devin hurried to the trailer and back. "Everyone puts these on now."

He put a surgeon's mask on his face and handed one each to Jen and Chris. Jen placed hers on and Devin tossed her a pair of latex gloves. "These, too."

Devin was the most animated she'd ever seen him. His brow furrowed and his posture stiffened. It took a minute before the reason hit her. The great Devin Reed was scared.

Devin picked up a shovel and handed it to Chris, who'd already donned his mask and gloves. "We have no idea what killed these men, but if it had anything to do with Leo's illness, we need to find out."

He headed back to the pit. "Jen, you're with me. Chris, bring the body bag out and spread it out on the ground."

He shined a flashlight at the edge of the pit, then stomped a foot along it. The ground remained solid. Jen peered into the grave. All of them had the same type of archaic clothes on. How long had they been there?

Devin pointed to the corpse of a bearded man in a cotton jacket and overalls. "Chris, point those two sidelights here."

When Chris had adjusted the lights, Devin lowered himself into the grave, almost tripping over a frozen leg. He waved Jen on. "Come."

She eased into the pit and placed her feet in the only two clear spots she could find. That's when the smell smacked her in the face. Nothing she'd ever encountered smelled as thick and as foul as the bodies and the thawing muck they lay in. She coughed and prayed she wouldn't puke in her mask.

Devin put a hand on her shoulder. "Easy. First time you've smelled something like this, isn't it?"

She nodded.

"It's the smell of death. Not the cleaned-up, funeral home kind of death, but the raw, unsanitized, natural version. It never leaves you once you experience it."

Jen breathed through her mouth. "Thanks for the warning."

Devin pointed at the bearded man. "What do you see?"

Jen coughed. "A smelly dead guy."

Devin sighed. "Get closer and look. You're a scientist, so act like one."

Jen frowned, but he was right. She took a deep breath

and bent down to examine the man. He looked to have been in his early thirties and was short, about five and a half feet. The fabric of the coat was torn down his entire left arm. She moved the torn fabric to the side and found a wound on his shoulder. "He's got a hell of a hickey here."

Devin squatted next to her and ran a gloved finger over the wound. "A bite."

Jen looked at him. "Is it possible some animals fed on these bodies?"

Chris stood on the edge of the pit, just above Devin, watching them. "Sure could. Grizzlies have been active lately."

Devin examined the bite. "Not big enough for a bear. Besides, this bite isn't recent. It was made before he died."

"How do you know that?" Chris asked.

Devin pointed at dried blood around the wound. "Wounds inflicted on a frozen body don't bleed."

The bearded man appeared to be atop the frozen soil and not trapped in it, so Jen pulled on his petrified arm to see if she could roll him over. She braced her right boot against another corpse's leg and pulled. The damn thing wasn't moving.

"Next time wait until I tell you to touch a body," Devin said. "This is an archaeological site and needs to be treated as such."

Jen felt heat rise in her cheeks. *Why am I always screwing up around him?* "OK."

Devin attempted to roll the corpse, but it didn't move for him, either. "In a normal dig we'd take days or weeks to carefully unearth a body, but Leo doesn't have that luxury, so we'll need to be a bit more brute force." He turned to Jen. "Grab a shovel. Chris, is that body bag ready?"

Chris's head popped up over the lip of the pit. He handed a shovel to Jen. "Ready when you are."

Jen tested the soil with the tip of her shovel. "Hard as a rock. We're not digging anybody out today."

Devin placed his shovel under the corpse's injured shoulder. "We don't have to get the shovels too far in, just enough to pry him up. Get yours under his upper thigh."

Jen jammed the tip of her shovel under the corpse's thigh. Devin pushed down on his shovel with his foot, driving the blade a couple inches into the permafrost. Jen did the same to hers, and it moved further under the body's thigh.

Devin wiped his brow. "You ready?"

Jen nodded.

Devin gripped the handle. "Ready, one, two, three."

Jen pushed down on her shovel. The corpse wasn't budging. Devin strained so much that tendons popped out in his neck.

The body raised a quarter inch. "Hold up," Devin said, letting go of his shovel.

"I think I have it." Jen grunted and pushed harder.

Just as she was about to give up, the body rolled over with a great ripping sound. The corpse's left arm tore off, still frozen into the ground.

Jen leaned on the shovel, panting. "Shit."

Devin threw his shovel down. "I told you to stop."

Jen took a deep breath and coughed. "If it helps, I don't think he felt a thing."

Devin put a hand to his forehead. "OK. OK. No big deal. Let's get him bagged and out of here."

Jen grabbed the corpse's legs. Devin had its upper body. They lifted and rolled it onto the body bag. Chris zipped it up while they climbed out of the pit. The three of them carried the body bag and placed it in the trailer, then threw in the shovels and went to get the lights.

Before turning hers off, Jen shined the lights further out into the pit. *What the hell?*

There were several body-shaped depressions, as if someone else had removed bodies, too. Who the hell would do that?

Devin called to her. "We've got everything packed except your lights."

Jen turned off the lights, plunging the pit back into darkness. She listened. Crackling and crunching like ice melting in a glass of tea. The tundra was thawing at an enormous rate.

She picked up the lamp and turned to bring it back to the trailer, but from somewhere not too far behind her came scratching sounds. She peered over her shoulder into the darkness, and the scratching stopped.

"Jen," Devin snapped. "Let's move."

Jen darted to the trailer and dropped the lamp off, then climbed onto her ATV and followed Chris the hell out of there.

6

After what seemed like hours, the shadowy outlines of Point Wallace houses appeared ahead. The sky had opened up again and the driving rain made it hard to see much detail beyond several yards. Jen adjusted her poncho hood in a doomed attempt at keeping the rain out of her eyes.

They wound their way through the village and climbed the hill, their tires working to gain traction.

"All this rain has softened the ground," Chris said. "There's more grass and less mud on the right side of the hill, so come up that way next time."

Lightning flashed, painting the trailers in momentary daylight.

Devin hopped off his ATV. "Let's get the body inside. Everything else can wait."

Devin held the science trailer door open as Jen and Chris stumbled inside with the body. He led them down the hallway to the archaeologist's room and gestured to the autopsy table. "On there."

He helped them lift the body onto the table and wiped

his hands on his pants. Jen felt filthy and wanted nothing more than a hot drink and a shower. "I'll go see if Pete has any coffee brewed."

She stepped into the hallway and almost collided with Hal. He tried to look past her and into the room. "What did you find?"

Jen moved aside and Devin waved Hal in. "A mass grave. The bodies are well preserved, but old. Late nineteenth century is my guess. We brought one back for examination."

Jen slipped back into the room. No way would she miss the conversation.

Hal removed his glasses and wiped them with a handkerchief. "I've got something as well, but I'm not exactly sure what it is. Want to take a look? It's over in the lab."

Devin nodded.

Hal strode from the room without a word, Devin on his heels.

Chris passed by Jen. "I'm going for that coffee."

"Catch you later." She hurried from the room and over to the lab trailer.

The lab looked as clean and antiseptic as it had when Hal had given them the tour earlier. Hal and Devin hovered over a microscope in the corner. Hal gave Devin an arched eyebrow when Jen joined them. Her heart skipped a beat. They weren't going to throw her out, were they? She was a scientist, too. Not as experienced or lauded as them, but so what?

Devin met Hal's gaze with an unblinking one of his own. "Whatever I can see, Jen can see."

Hal shrugged, and Jen let out a breath. Devin was really trying to connect with her. It wasn't quite enough for her to forget his years of absences, but she felt a connection to him she hadn't before.

Hal pulled a vial of blood from a small refrigerator beneath the table. He tilted it so one drop landed on a glass slide, then pressed another slide onto it and placed them under the stage clips.

Hal peered into the eyepiece and adjusted the focus. "I wasn't sure what I was seeing at first." He straightened and stepped back. "Take a look."

Devin looked into the microscope. "Looks normal to me."

He straightened and motioned Jen over. She peered through the eyepiece and saw hundreds of donut-shaped red blood cells. "Same here."

"Watch closer," Hal said. "The outer boundaries of the cells."

Jen squinted and adjusted the focus. It took a minute, but she found a cell with a membrane that didn't look right. "Looks like it's blackening."

"Keep watching," Hal said. "Now that you've found one, you should see more."

He was right. She noticed dozens of cells in the same condition. The blackening of the membrane seemed to be spreading. She straightened and let Devin look. "What the hell is it?"

"It's not bacterial," Hal said. "We'd see that. My guess is some type of virus."

Devin looked up from the microscope. "You can't see it?"

Hal removed the slides, placed them in a plastic bag, and sealed it with tape. He tossed it in a biohazard waste bucket. "As well supplied as we are, we don't have an electron microscope." He rubbed his eyes. "Besides, I'm no virologist. We'll have to get the samples to Anchorage once the weather clears. There's an associate of mine, Dr. Wilson, who's staging labs for a new study on the effects of cold temperatures on the human body. He has contacts in the CDC." He sighed. "But for now I have nothing new to help Leo."

Devin clasped him on the shoulder. "You've done what you can."

"No." Hal strode toward the trailer door. "I haven't. Let's take a closer look at that body you brought in."

Jen jogged to keep up with Hal and Devin. "Not much you can do with a frozen body."

Hal ignored her. She followed them into the headquarters trailer. Hal stopped at the admin office door. Pete sat at his desk, shuffling papers, while Chris leaned against the wall, coffee mug in hand, talking to him.

"Still no radio?" Hal asked.

Pete shook his head. "I gave up for now."

"Keep trying," Hal said. "We may have a contagion, and need to let the state authorities know. They can contact the CDC and get the ball rolling."

Pete's eyebrows rose. "Contagion?"

Hal nodded. "Just a precaution, but Leo's blood may contain a virus, so we need to play it safe. And the logical place for him to have contracted it would be at the mass grave."

Chris frowned. "So are we infected, too?"

"Doubtful," Hal said. "I suspect Leo got it from his wound. Most likely, it's not airborne, but passed on through fluids."

Jen pursed her lips. Hal was making a lot of assumptions. Did he believe what he said, or was he just trying to keep everyone calm? "What good does it do to tell Wainwright? It's not like they can get the state troopers or anything."

"They might," Pete said. "They have newer and more

powerful radio equipment and can cut through outages we don't have a hope to."

"And now I'm going to check our friend on the autopsy table," Hal said. "Devin, Jen. With me."

They returned to the archaeologist's office. Devin rummaged through the boxes, pulling supplies. He handed Jen and Hal long rubber aprons, masks, and gloves. He donned his own set and laid a selection of scalpels and syringes on the table next to the body bag.

Hal unzipped the bag and turned on the overhead surgical light. "Let's take a look at our mystery man."

Jen stood on the other side of the table as Hal pulled the bag back to reveal the corpse's face. Other than the slightly grayish tinge of the skin, he looked as if he were sleeping.

Hal tried to pry the eyelids open. "They're still frozen."

He looked at Devin. "What do you make of the clothes? Seen anything like this before?"

Devin looked closely at the corpse's coat. "Coarse wool. Almost like a pea coat." He unfastened a button. "Black glass buttons. Most likely this gentleman is from the late 1800s, as I thought." He unbuttoned the rest of the coat and opened it.

Piles of brown dust were stacked up on the man's shirt, his underarms, and in the inside folds of the coat. Jen reached out and pinched some between her gloved fingers.

"What is it?" Devin asked.

Jen rubbed the dust. She'd seen something similar a year before. It turned out to be tiny, almost microscopic, spores. *But where did they come from?* "It's very fine. Could be a lot of things, but I'd need to see it under a microscope to tell for sure."

Devin rummaged through a box on the shelf. He removed a small capped plastic vial, opened it, and held it out to Jen. She picked up more dust and dropped it into the vial. He closed it and handed it to her.

Hal felt the dead man's temples. "Not much we can do on this frozen end. Let's check the extremities."

He spread the bag more, exposing an arm. He lifted the wrist and flexed it. "Better." He moved the fingers. "Fingers thawed, pliable." He glanced over his shoulder. "Can you hand me the heavy scissors?"

Jen stepped next to him, selected the scissors from the array of tools, and handed them over.

Hal cut the heavy wool of the coat arm and then the cotton shirt sleeve, exposing a hairy arm with a crude tattoo of a woman in a grass skirt. "Definitely a sailor."

Devin nodded. "As far as I could see, all the other bodies were dressed the same."

Hal pressed on the underside of the forearm. "Hand me the syringe. I've found a spot thawed enough to penetrate."

Jen handed him a syringe, and he inserted its long needle into the arm and pulled the plunger back. Deep dark red blood filled the barrel. He placed it to the side and zipped up the body bag. Pulling down his mask, he let out a long breath. "Let's go to the lab and see what we can make of this."

He strode into the hallway, with Devin following.

Jen stepped out of the room and removed her mask. Chris leaned against the wall with his arms crossed. "So what do we have?"

She wiped a hand across her forehead. "Besides a hundred-and-twenty-year-old popsicle that smells like fish? We've got a bit of a mystery. Who were these guys and how did they get there?" She nodded at him. "How long has this village been here?"

Chris shrugged. "Thousands of years."

"And there's no mention of these sailors in your stories?"

"No. So they are sailors?"

"Yeah, from the late 1800s, most likely."

"We can ask my uncle. He might know, but I'd be surprised. Our stories are passed on from generation to generation. They aren't meant to be secret. On the contrary, it's important to us that they be shared."

"It could be important," Jen said. "I've got to get to the lab, but maybe you should find your uncle and join us there."

Chris nodded. "See you there." He ran off.

When Jen got to the lab, Hal was bent over the microscope. He sat up, removed his glasses, and rubbed the bridge of his nose. "Same thing as Leo."

Devin took a look. "Sure is. Guess that solves the puzzle of how Leo became infected."

Jen took a clean slide and spread some of the dust on it. "Let's see what we have here."

She sat at the microscope and swapped slides. Closing one eye, she squinted into the eyepiece and adjusted the focus. It zoomed in to show clusters of spiny shaped spores. "Scleroderma areolatum."

"What was that?" Devin asked.

Jen straightened. "Spiny spores."

"Is that significant?" Hal asked.

Jen dropped the capped vial of spores into her shirt pocket. "Not sure. Would love to study them on an electron microscope."

A metallic *chunk chunk* came from the doorway. Having spent a lot of time at the gun range, Jen knew exactly what that was.

She spun. A short elderly native man with salt-and-pepper hair hanging wildly down to his shoulders aimed a twelve gauge shotgun at them.

No one moved. The man pointed the gun at each one of them in turn. "Where is the Tuqunaragri?"

Jen and Devin looked at each other. What the hell was he talking about? Jen's pulse pounded her ears, but still her mouth opened before she knew it. "I'll bet we can find it for you on Google maps."

The wild man squinted at her.

Shit. When will I learn to shut up?

Hal's voice quivered. "We don't understand that word."

The man squeezed his eyes shut for a moment. "The body you brought back from Fear Mountain. The Tuqunaragri. Either you take it back now, or you'll join it."

7

Jen stared at the shotgun, her mouth going dry. *Am I going to die in this place?*

Devin put his hands up and spoke in a calm, soothing voice. How he managed that, Jen would never know.

"Put the gun down and we can talk."

The man swung the shotgun to point at Devin. "The body must go back now, before it's too late."

Devin took a deep breath. "We can do that. Just put the gun down."

Raymond appeared in the doorway behind the man, towering over him. "What are you doing, Norman?"

Norman spun and spoke to Raymond in Inupiaq. Raymond answered him in kind and held his hands out. The man gave him the gun. Jen let out a breath she hadn't known she was holding.

Raymond stepped into the room. "What's this all about?"

Norman answered, again in Inupiaq. Raymond shook his head and put a hand up. "In English."

Norman looked from Raymond to the others, and back

again, his lips a thin line across his face. For a few moments there was silence, then his shoulders sagged and he nodded. "It's time to tell the story."

Raymond laid the shotgun on a table. "What story?"

"The story of Fear Mountain."

Jen's heart rate had slowed to near normal, but her legs were wobbly, so she pulled out a stool and sat.

Norman closed his eyes for a moment, then spoke. "The story passes down that in the latter part of the 1800s, they came. I've since looked up some of the known facts on the Internet and found that in 1871 a fleet of thirty-three whaling ships was trapped in the ice. The sea had frozen all the way to land as close as a few miles north of here. We knew nothing of it at the time, until men walked off the ice and into our village. They staggered and moved very slowly, as if they had frozen limbs from their journey. Our elders approached them, but as they got closer and the strange men saw the elders, the strangers let forth a terrible sound. These men, these ice walkers, had deep yellow eyes, and they growled and gnashed their teeth as they came. Had their limbs not been half frozen, they surely would've caught the elders."

Raymond frowned. "And you're saying these ice walkers are the same men whose bodies Leo found?"

Norman nodded. He pointed at Devin. "The same as the one he brought back to the village. A Tuqunaragri."

Jen stood, but kept a steadying hand on the table next to her. "What does that mean?"

Raymond scratched his head and squinted. "The literal translation is one who acts dead."

A chill ran down Jen's spine and her mind flashed back to the scratching she'd heard in the pit. Maybe the old guy wasn't crazy.

Devin crossed his arms. "All legends have a grain of truth. Perhaps these men were just sick. If I recall, there was a large typhoid outbreak during that time."

Norman shrugged. "I don't know. I only tell you what has been passed down. In it was the warning that they would destroy the world if they were ever disturbed. This is why we have the stories of spirits at Fear Mountain—to keep everyone away."

Hal took off his glasses and wiped them on his shirt. "If those bodies at Fear Mountain are the same ones you describe, how did they get out there? How did they get buried?"

"Another ship docked, here at our village. Men from the government, Army men and men who were in charge that did not wear uniforms, came ashore. By then the bodies had frozen completely in the subzero temperatures and stood like statues all around the village and beyond. These men collected the bodies and moved them out to Fear Mountain. The tundra was hard to dig in, so they set up large tents and built fires underneath them to thaw the ground enough to dig. Many men worked in shifts for days and dug a trench, a pit. They tossed the bodies in and filled it. Because of the permafrost, these creatures would stay frozen forever."

Raymond shook his head. "Why have I not heard this before?"

Norman licked his lips. "When they had buried the bodies, the men from the government, the ones not in uniform, spoke to the elders. They said that no one must know of this, and if word ever got out, then our village would be destroyed. So the elders called a meeting and everyone pledged to silence. As the new generation was born, none knew about this, and the older generations died off. But they didn't want it completely forgotten in case the information was useful to our people someday, so there were always three elders who knew the story. When an elder that knew died off, the other two would pick a replacement and burden them with the secret."

"Who are the other two elders?" Raymond asked.

"Jacob Adams and your mother."

"My mother?"

Norman nodded. "We were all sworn to secrecy. When your mother passes, we plan on you taking her place."

"I see," Raymond said. "Norman, will you go to my house and help my mother take care of Leo?"

"What about the Tuqunaragri?"

"Let me talk it over with Hal and his friends. We'll figure out the best way to get the body back."

Norman stared at Raymond for a few moments, then turned and trudged out the door.

Raymond nodded at Hal. "So what have you been able to find out about Leo's illness?"

Hal cleared his throat. "Leo's blood has some anomalies."

"Anomalies? What does that mean?"

Jen crossed her arms. *Enough talking around it.* "There's something wrong with their blood cells, and Leo has the same problem. He was infected when he was impaled on the bone."

Raymond frowned. "Is that true? What is the cure?"

"I don't know." Hal's shoulders lowered. "It's something I've never seen before."

Jen sighed. "I know what to do. We need to get Leo to Wainwright. The weather is lightening up. Maybe the radio's working now?"

Chris walked into the room. "There you all are. I've been looking for you." He looked at Jen, then his gaze went to the shotgun on the table. "What's going on?"

Raymond put a hand on his shoulder. "We'll fill you in later, but we've got to get Leo to Wainwright."

"Wainwright's a long way," Chris said.

Hal cleared his throat. "This is way beyond me. He may not survive the trip, but it's his only hope."

Jen walked to the doorway. "I'll see if Pete's making progress."

"That's why I came over here," Chris said. "Pete made contact with Wainwright for less than a minute. He told them about the contagion, but isn't sure if they got it or not."

Hal pulled the truck keys out of his pocket. "I'd better get back and take a look at Leo. Anyone coming?"

Devin stood. "Let me check on our guest on the autopsy table, and I'll be right out. I just want to make sure Norman didn't do anything to him."

Jen followed him out.

THE CORPSE APPEARED UNDISTURBED. Devin and Jen put on gloves, and Jen unzipped the body bag. Devin lifted the sailor's arm and bent it, while Jen did the same with a leg.

"His arm has a lot more flexibility," Devin said.

Jen nodded. "So do his legs. In fact, he's pretty damn limber for a man who's been dead over a hundred years."

"He's thawing fast." Devin felt the sailor's head. "But the head's still frozen. It'll probably be the last part to thaw."

He zipped the bag closed and took off his gloves. Jen snapped hers off, tossed them in the biohazard box, and headed out to the truck. It was running and everyone else was in it when they arrived. Jen squeezed in next to Chris and Raymond in the back, while Devin hopped in the front. Jen caught Chris up with what he'd missed as they rode to Raymond's.

When they arrived, Hal jumped out, grabbed his bag, and jogged up the steps. He opened the door and froze. Jen stopped behind him. "What's wrong?"

When Hal didn't answer, she peered around him. Raymond's mother lay on the kitchen floor. Her chest looked like it had exploded, painting the walls and the floor around her in blood. Her entrails hung out of her abdominal cavity and were spread across the tiles. The place smelled like a freezer full of meat that'd gone bad.

"What the hell?" Devin's voice came from behind her.

Norman, the elder with the shotgun fetish, lay on the couch, a slack expression on his face. Leo leaned over him with his back to the front door. Ripping and chewing sounds came from him. Norman's hand rose weakly. "Help me," he moaned.

Jen's mind slipped gears as she tried to make sense of the scene in front of her, but Raymond broke her trance. "Mother."

Raymond pushed past the others and rushed to his mother. Slipping on the gore, he landed on his back beside her. He scrambled to his knees, sobbing.

Hal staggered backward onto the porch, his face bloodless.

Leo spun, his yellow eyes glowing with hate. Blood stained his face and dripped onto his chest, and he chewed what looked like a piece of intestine. He dropped it and screeched, "Scree!"

Jen cringed. It was the sound of nails running across a chalkboard, and it went right through her. Bile rose in her throat and she was frozen to the spot, clamping her hands over her ears.

With a primal growl, Leo leapt on her.

8

Leo slammed into Jen and drove her to the floor, knocking the air from her lungs. She managed to jam her elbow against his throat and kept his gnashing teeth inches away from her face. His breath had the rotten stink of the pit. She tried to catch her breath and gagged.

Devin kicked Leo's side. "Get off my daughter!"

Leo ignored him and pressed farther, his snapping jaw closer and closer to Jen. She had to do something or he would tear her face apart. She tried to raise her knees, get them underneath him so she could shove him off, but his weight was too much. He was going to eat her face.

The pressure on her elbow disappeared, and Leo was pulled off, Raymond and Chris each grasping one of his arms. Leo struggled like a feral cat, trying to bite them as they dragged him back to the couch.

Jen rolled up onto all fours, shuddering and coughing. Devin took her arm and helped her stand. Her knees buckled, and he kept her from falling by wrapping an arm around her. Raymond had Leo's arms pinned behind him, and while Leo kicked and growled, his yellow eyes drilled into Jen's.

"Everyone out," Raymond yelled. "Get ready to close the door once I've cleared it."

Devin led Jen out. Fresh air slapped her in the face, giving her strength. Hal leaned over the porch rail, puking onto the muddy road.

Chris stationed himself beside the open door. "Ready when you are, Uncle Raymond."

Raymond's voice came from the house. "I'm coming on the count of three. Close the door after I get through."

Devin leaned Jen against the rail. "Are you okay by yourself?"

Jen nodded, and Devin stationed himself next to Chris.

"One, two, three!" A crash came from inside the house, and Raymond streaked through the doorway. Devin and Chris rammed their shoulders into the door and slammed it shut. The door shuddered as a heavy weight hit it from the other side.

Raymond ran back to the door, his keys in hand, and locked the deadbolt. He leaned with his back against the house, breathing heavily, his arms and shirt stained with blood. "What the hell's wrong with him?"

Hal straightened, still clutching the railing. "Leo needs help."

Jen's legs felt less rubbery, and she stumbled toward the others. "Help? Leo needs a straitjacket."

Raymond shot her a dirty look. Chris put his hand on his uncle's shoulder. "You OK?"

Raymond nodded.

"We need to get out of here," Devin said.

Raymond's brow furrowed. "I'm not leaving my nephew or my village."

Hal frowned. "I don't want to bring the infection elsewhere."

"But Wainwright's radio equipment can get through when ours can't," Jen said. "Isn't that what Pete told us?"

"True." Hal tapped a finger on his chin and stared off into space. "And even if we have the virus, we'd get the CDC involved quicker from Wainwright, and prevent it from spreading any further."

Jen straightened, much steadier than before. "Then Devin and I can go to Wainwright and send the message."

"You'll never make it there alive," Raymond said. "Not by yourselves."

Chris raised his hand. "I can take them, then bring their medic back for Leo."

"It's probably our best chance," Hal said.

The banging stopped. Raymond pressed his ear against the door. "He's still there, but he's breathing awfully heavy. I hope he doesn't hurt himself."

Jen raised an eyebrow. "Not exactly on the top of my worry list."

Raymond looked at Hal and sighed. "You're probably right. It's the best chance we have."

Hal headed for the truck. "I'm going with you, since there's nothing I can do for Leo at this point. Let's get moving."

THIRTY MINUTES LATER, Jen and Devin stood next to four ATVs in front of the science trailers. Devin put a hand on Jen's shoulder, concern written on his face. She remembered how he'd attacked Leo to save her. "I'll get you out of here," he said. "I may not have been there for you when you were growing up, but I'm here now."

Jen's eyes searched his, her lips pressed tightly together and she swallowed. "We'll get each other out of here."

Devin smiled. "That's a deal."

Hal and Chris came out of the trailer with four backpacks. Chris handed one to Jen. "Food and water for the trip."

They loaded up and started off down the hill with Chris leading. As they weaved slowly through the village, they passed Raymond's house. He stood on the porch, his hands raised, and talked to a group of villagers gathered before him. It looked as if he were calming them down.

Outside of town Chris sped up, and the others kept pace, their headlights lighting up the terrain ahead of them. Even though the rain had stopped, the cloud cover had thickened, casting the tundra in a deeper gloom.

They stopped at the break in the trail. Jen looked toward the mountain. She couldn't see it in the dark, but she could feel it.

Chris turned to the others. "We need to go inland, but not all the way to the mountain."

Devin nodded. "That's good by me. I don't need to run into that place again in the dark."

Chris sped off with the others following. A few minutes in, he turned right. Although bumpy, the ground seemed more solid to Jen than it had during their last trip. They maintained a moderate speed, and Jen had already started wondering how long the trip would take when a man staggered into the headlight beams, directly in front of Chris. Chris swerved, missing the man by inches, and Jen got a flash of the man's face. Ashen skin, facial hair, yellow eyes. *Impossible.*

A dozen more men lumbered toward them from three sides. Chris signaled the others to stop.

The man Chris had nearly hit tilted his head to the sky and let out an ear-piercing screech. *Just like Leo.* The other men answered in kind and they all staggered in an almost-jog toward the riders.

Screeches echoed from the darkness around them. They seemed to come from hundreds of voices and from every direction. Jen screamed over the cacophony. "We need to get the hell out of here."

Hal yelled over the engines. "There's an opening in their ranks. If we can get through there, we'll have a clear path to Wainwright. Come on."

He gunned his throttle and roared between two groups of sailors. Just as he shot by them, his headlights lit up a dense wall of more sailors in front of him. Hal's brake lights flared, but he didn't stop in time and slammed into them, sending sailor bodies flying. Hal tried to turn the ATV around, but one of the creatures bear hugged him from behind and bit into his neck.

"Hal," Devin yelled.

Hal screamed. Blood spurted from his neck and sprayed other sailors, who pounced on him, dragging him to the ground as they fed.

An ashen hand clutched Jen's shoulder. *Oh, shit.* Jen accelerated, but the sailor hung on as the ATV shot out from under her. Slammed to the ground, she gasped.

The sailor bent down toward her, his mouth open and ready to bite. She kicked his chest with both legs, sending him flying back, then hopped to her feet. More sailors had locked onto her and weren't far away, and the guy she'd kicked was getting back up. *I should've at least knocked the wind out of him.*

A beeping horn caught her attention and she spun. Two sets of headlights zoomed toward her. Chris zipped past and ran into the nearest sailor, knocking him back. Devin came to a skidding stop and she jumped on behind him, wrapping her arms around his waist. "Let's get the hell out of here."

Devin followed Chris as they raced back the way they'd come. Jen glanced over her shoulder. The mass of sailors had turned and were lumbering after them. *We're leading them right to the village.*

9

Hal's death played over and over in Jen's mind. It had happened so fast. *What a gruesome way to die.* She clenched her jaw. She'd be damned if she and Devin would end up like him.

The village came into view, with some houses lit from a porch light or a glow through a window, and others nothing more than a black silhouette in the distance.

A figure ran from the village and onto the tundra. Another figure burst from behind a house, sprinted after the first one, and jumped on it like a lion bringing down its prey.

What the hell? No way the dead could've beat them back.

They entered the village and stopped in front of Raymond's house. The streets were deserted, and a quiet cloaked the scene. No rain. No thunder. No lightning. Just the wind and oppressing darkness.

Chris hopped off his four-wheeler and grabbed his rifle from the gun scabbard. Keeping his voice low, he said, "I need to find Uncle Raymond."

Jen dismounted. Sweat ran down the back of her neck. *Where is everyone?*

She followed Chris onto Raymond's porch. The front door was splintered open from the inside, and fresh blood had pooled on the rubber welcome mat. "I'll come with you," she said.

Devin grabbed her arm. "We don't know what's in there."

A woman's scream came from somewhere toward the hill, followed by a chorus of screeches from all directions.

Jen licked her lips. "I think we know what's out here. Besides, we should stick together."

Chris nodded. "You two come inside and watch the door. I'll search the house for Uncle Raymond."

"OK." Devin stepped inside and stood against the wall on one side of the doorway. Jen took the other side, wrinkling her nose at the overpowering smell of rancid meat. Chris crept into the shadows of the living room and disappeared.

A screech came from a house a block away. A woman ran out the front door, pursued by a child whose yellow eyes caught the light from an open door across the street. The little girl growled and snapped her teeth as she raced after the woman. She wrapped her arms around the woman's leg and bit into her calf, dragging her down. The girl crawled up the writhing woman's back and bit into her shoulder, pulling a chunk of flesh out and chewing it like a piece of steak.

A bang came from the back of the house. Jen pressed into the wall, peering into the blackness of the living room. *We're surrounded.*

The floor squeaked, and Chris stepped from the darkness of the hallway. "No one here."

Jen let out the lungful of air she hadn't realized she'd been holding in. "You scared the shit out of me."

Devin slumped into a sitting position and put a hand to his forehead. "Phew."

Rifle slung over his shoulder, Chris carried a handgun and a three-foot section of metal pipe. "Didn't find Uncle Raymond, but I did pick these up."

Chris handed Devin the gun. Devin held it away like it would explode at any second. "I don't know what to do with this."

"I do." Jen took it from Devin, and he gaped as she removed the magazine, slammed it back in, and pulled the slide back, letting it snap forward. "Sig .45. Nice."

"You know guns?" Devin asked.

Jen frowned. "You don't spend a lot of time in the Alaskan outdoors without one." She held the pistol up. "I'll take this."

Chris shrugged and handed Devin the pipe. "Low tech, but it packs a punch."

Chris handed two boxes of ammo to Jen. She opened them and dumped the rounds into her pockets. "I'm ready."

They stepped out of the house, and the zombie kid looked up from its dinner. Blood sprayed from its mouth as it screeched.

Chris aimed the rifle at it, but didn't pull the trigger. He lowered the barrel. "That's little Annie Brower. I've watched her for her folks a time or two. I can't shoot her. She's just a kid."

Annie streaked toward them, teeth bared and an animal growl rumbling in her throat. Devin raised the pipe over his head. Jen aimed the Sig and pulled the trigger. The bullet hit Annie in the chest and she staggered, then fell forward on her hands and knees. Heart hammering, Jen lowered the gun. *I just killed a little girl.*

Devin lowered the pipe. "God help us all."

Annie's head rose, her piercing yellow eyes fixed on Jen. She sprinted at her as if she'd never been shot. Annie reached the porch steps and leapt. Jen pumped two more shots into her, one in the chest and the other in the stomach. Annie dropped onto the steps, then sprung again. The pipe flashed by Jen and bashed Annie's temple—a hollow gong rang out when it connected. She dropped to the porch in a heap and lay still.

Jen kept the gun pointed at her. "Is the zombie dead?"

Devin squinted. "Zombie?"

Chris prodded Annie with the barrel of his rifle, rolling her over. "Might as well call it what it is." Annie's head was caved in at the left temple. "Seems to be really dead this time. Poor Annie."

A growl from the street behind them caused Jen to spin. Annie's victim had risen and glowered at them with predator's eyes. Two villagers streaked past the porch, followed by another raging zombie. The zombie's stomach was ripped open, frayed ends of its guts trailing behind it and flapping in the wind. The villagers disappeared behind a house. Just before he followed, the zombie looked back at Annie's victim and light splashed on him. His face was ashen, and his long hair even more scraggly than the last time Jen had seen him. *Norman.*

Norman screeched and ran off after his prey. Annie's victim followed.

Devin gripped the pipe tighter. "We've got to find a safe place. Get out of the open."

Jen shivered. "After what we've just seen, there might not be a safe place."

10

Chris wiped his forehead with the back of his hand. "Uncle Raymond would either go to the science trailers or the community center."

Jen checked her ammo. "I'm not feeling warm fuzzies that a trailer would keep those things out. Besides, the community center's that big building we passed, isn't it? It looked pretty sturdy, and it's only a couple of blocks away."

Chris stepped off the porch, his head on a swivel, looking back and forth. "Follow me."

Jen nodded toward Chris. "Follow him. I'll take up the rear. That'll keep the guns in front and back."

Devin hesitated. He looked like he would say something, but then hurried after Chris.

Chris led them to the shadows of the building across the street. He snuck to the corner and peered around, then whispered, "The door's closed, so that's a good sign, but there are four zombies milling around in front of it."

Devin rubbed his chin. "We need a diversion. If we can pull them away from the door, we have a chance."

"We should move up a building," Chris said. "That'll put

us only twenty yards away. I think we can do it without being seen, just be real quiet."

He stepped around the corner and crept forward, staying in the shadows, Devin right behind him. Another zombie stumbled onto the road, but didn't turn Jen's way. She slipped around the corner and followed the others to the next house, glancing over her shoulder to make sure they weren't followed.

A zombie screech in the distance ripped through the night, followed by several gunshots. The zombies in front of the community center all tilted their heads back and returned the call. They ran off in the direction of the original screech.

Jen hugged the wall. Other screeches answered from all directions. Dozens of zombies streaked past the end of the road, oblivious to the prey nearby.

How many new zombies are there now?

One zombie turned its head and stared at her as it raced by. No doubt it had seen her. Why didn't it stop?

Jen put a hand to her pounding chest. "They swarm like bees."

Chris squatted and felt around, then stood, holding an empty bottle. "But did they all go? Let's see if there are any left close by."

Jen put an arm out to stop him. "Wait."

Chris stepped to the edge of the house and flung the bottle. It landed with a crash between two houses across the way. Nearby screeches echoed from several directions.

The blood drained from Jen's face. "Shit. That's going to bring a swarm. Go."

Chris raced toward the community center doors. Devin stumbled, caught his balance, and hurried after Chris. Jen swept the area with her gun. No targets yet. She darted toward the community center and was halfway there when Chris got to the doors and tried opening them.

Chris looked back at her, his face drawn. "Locked."

Devin arrived and pulled on the handle. No good.

A screech from close behind her sent chills over Jen's body. She dug in her heels and pumped her arms, giving it all she had. Chris and Devin banged on the door. "Let us in. It's Chris."

Several more screeches rang out. *Thanks for throwing the damn bottle, Chris.*

One of the double doors flew open, and Raymond stood in the doorway. He stepped back, raised a shotgun, and aimed it past Jen. She hoped he was a good shot.

Chris ducked into the building, but Devin stood, looking behind Jen, his eyes wide. "Run! They're right behind you."

Jen waved at him to go on. With a frown on his face, he backed into the building, holding the pipe at the ready. Raymond fired. The thump of a body hitting the ground behind her spurred Jen into one last burst of speed. She streaked through the doorway and tripped, falling and sliding across the shiny linoleum floor. She came to a stop on her back, panting. Her gaze snapped to the open door. A dozen zombies had almost reached it. Raymond and Chris slammed the door closed, and Raymond propped a bar against it. The door shuddered from the impact of the zombies, but it held.

An elderly villager with jumbled white hair and a vacant look in her eyes scuffled over to Jen. "Have you seen my sister Gwen? I've been looking all over for her."

Raymond put an arm around the woman's shoulder and led her away. "Come on, Tara. Let's get you a comfortable chair."

Chris held out a hand and helped Jen up. "What's with

her?" Jen asked.

"Tara has dementia," Chris said. "Her sister takes care of her. She's lost without her."

"Where is her sister?" Jen asked.

Chris scanned the room. "I don't see her in here."

Raymond returned. "Can someone tell me what the hell's going on around here?"

Devin shook his head, panting. "Some type of contagion. Has to be what Leo has."

"Contagion?" Raymond let out a nervous laugh. "That turns people into monsters?"

Jen brushed her pants off. "They're zombies."

Raymond gawked at her.

Even with all that's happened, he's looking at me as if I'm crazy?

"Yes, Uncle," Chris said. "People die and come back to eat the living."

"Zombies?" Raymond looked at Devin. "I know what I've seen looks like zombies, but you're a scientist. Surely there's another explanation."

Devin sighed. "I don't know what to believe, but the creatures do act like zombies you'd see in books and movies, and since there's no scientific term for them, zombies will do."

Raymond scratched his head, then looked around. "Speaking of science, where's Hal?"

"He was eaten by the zombies you don't believe in," Jen said.

Raymond's eyebrows rose. "What?"

"The dead sailors in the pit," Jen said. "And they're heading this way."

"Oh, shit." Raymond paced. "How many?"

"If they all reanimated," Devin said, "a couple hundred at least, but we never saw the full extent of the pit."

Jen looked around the room at the clusters of villagers, most of whom had a blank look on their face, as if they'd just woken up from a nightmare. *Or to a nightmare.* "That would be more of them than the humans in here. What do we have? Fifty? Sixty?"

"Forty-eight at last count," Raymond said. "That's out of a population of two hundred seventy-one."

The banging on the door intensified, causing it to shudder. Raymond slammed a fist into his hand. "Another fifty of those things on that door and it'll crack like an eggshell. Two hundred more and there'll be no place to hide."

Chris cleared his throat. "What happened here, Uncle?"

"Leo broke through and attacked us," he said. "He bit a chunk out of old Simeon's neck, then ran off. Simeon was pumping blood all over the place and died. A couple minutes later, he jumped up and his eyes had turned yellow, just like Leo. He grabbed his sister and chewed on her arm." Raymond sighed. "It all went to shit from there. A bunch of us came here and locked the doors. We've been able to get a few people in, but only a few."

Chris put an arm around his uncle. "You saved people. That's what matters."

Raymond shrugged. "But for how long? These creatures keep finding people hiding in their houses and attack them. Their numbers are growing."

A shout came from across the room. Tara peered out a window and waved. "Gwen is out there. She looks hurt."

She ran to a side door. "I need to let her in."

"Tara! No!" Raymond sprinted toward her, with Devin, Jen, and Chris on his heels.

Tara flung the door open, her arms wide. "Gwen. Over here."

A chorus of screeches answered her.

11

Chris sprinted past the others and reached the door just as an obese middle-aged woman in a kuspuk darted in and leapt on Tara. Chris rammed his shoulder into the door and slammed it home.

Tara's screams cut off into a watery gurgle as Gwen bent down and clamped her mouth on Tara's lips. It looked like she was giving her mouth-to-mouth. But Gwen pulled back, shaking her head viciously, and ripped Tara's lips off her face. The zombie stood, chewing the flesh and swallowing as Raymond slid to a stop before her. Gritting his teeth, he leveled the shotgun and fired. The pellets shredded the kuspuk and turned the zombie's stomach to hamburger. She snarled at Raymond and lunged. He gripped the shotgun at both ends and barely kept her from his throat by pressing it against her chest.

Devin swung the pipe and it glanced off the zombie's head. The damn thing stumbled backward, releasing its grip on Raymond.

The head. That's how Dad killed Annie. "Hit her in the head," Jen yelled. "It's the only way to stop them."

Chris swung his rifle around and fired. Half of Gwen's head disintegrated in a red spray, and she fell in a heap.

Raymond wiped his brow. "How'd you know how to kill them?"

Devin panted, his hand on his chest. "Brilliant, Jen." He looked at Raymond. "I killed one on your porch with a blow to the head. And that was after it had taken several bullets to the body."

Devin spun as a screech came from behind him. Tara came to her feet, her yellow eyes glaring at him. Tongue flicking from a ruined mouth, she crouched, ready to attack.

Jen only had one chance. She took the firing position she'd been taught in firearms class, aimed over her dad's shoulder, and squeezed the trigger. A hole appeared in Tara's forehead, and the back of her head exploded, spraying blood, flesh, and bone across the linoleum floor. She dropped like a marionette whose strings had been cut.

Devin whirled and said something to Jen. With a ringing in her ears, she yelled, "Can't hear."

He hugged her and spoke into her ear. "Thanks for the assist."

She squeezed him. "No charge for the first one. Besides, we're getting each other out of this, right?"

"That's right."

Chris's head hung. "Poor Tara. She deserved better."

Jen's gut ached. She'd been celebrating killing a zombie, while Chris considered it to still be Tara. She put a hand on his shoulder. "I'm sorry. I forgot these are people you grew up with. I didn't mean to be cruel."

"Not your fault," Chris said. "If I don't get over it and start taking these things out myself, more of my friends will die."

Devin nodded. "It's unfortunate, but you have to consider your friends gone once they turn."

Chris managed a weak smile. "You're right. Jen saved our lives. I shouldn't be whining." He gave Jen a thumbs up. "That was a heck of a shot."

Jen squeezed his shoulder. *Need to change the subject.* "Thanks, but did you notice that bitten people are turning faster? Leo took hours. This last one took a couple of minutes."

"The virus may be mutating," Devin said.

"Listen up," Raymond bellowed. "No doors get opened without my permission. I don't care who you see out there." The men and women who'd stood off to the side during the attack mumbled and nodded.

Raymond motioned to Chris. "Find those who still have their wits and station one person at each door." Chris ran off to a group of men gathered in front of the restrooms. A few of the men nodded and headed for the doors.

Chris jogged back over. "All the doors are covered."

Raymond walked to the middle of the room and clapped his hands sharply together. The villagers went silent, the constant banging and growling at the door the only sound. "Last we heard, the storm's supposed to break tonight. Our weekly supply plane is scheduled to arrive in the morning. So we just need to last the night."

The villagers murmured among themselves. Raymond went on. "But we need to be able to defend ourselves. So I want everyone to grab a weapon. Anything hefty that you can swing and knock these things in the head. That's the key. Any other damage doesn't bring them down, only the head."

Three men and a woman walked up to Raymond and pulled out handguns. Raymond nodded. "Good. I'd like each of you to double up with a door guard."

"What about me?"

Raymond spun. Griffin, the bootlegger, stood patting the grip of a long-barreled revolver holstered on his hip.

"What've you got?" Raymond asked.

".357 Magnum."

Chris's eyebrows rose. "Bad-ass gun." He pointed to Griffin's other hip. "What's that, a hatchet?"

Griffin removed the weapon from the sheath attached to his belt. "Tactical tomahawk. Small, but deadly."

"You're sober?" Raymond asked.

"As can be."

Arms crossed, Raymond stared into Griffin's eyes. "You stay here so you can back up any of the doors."

Griffin nodded. "You got it."

Villagers overturned chairs and broke the legs off. One man took the axe hanging next to the fire extinguisher and gave it a few practice swings. In the midst of all this, the banging and growling at the doors grew louder.

Shattering glass sounded from the women's room. Chris flung the door open. Three zombies had broken the window and were feasting on a woman lying on the floor, her throat ripped out and her glassy eyes staring at the ceiling. Another zombie lunged for Chris. Jen shot it in the face, blowing off its lower jaw, but not stopping it. *Shit.* Her second round went in its left eye, and it dropped. Chris slammed the door shut and pressed his back against it. Jen and Raymond helped him as the door shuddered under the zombie attack.

"Bring us something to brace this door," Chris yelled. A man rushed over with a two by four, jammed one end under the doorknob, and braced the other end against the floor. It slipped. Raymond grimaced. "The linoleum's too slick."

Jen waved to the man with the axe. "Bring that over here."

The man with the axe ran over. "Give it to Chris," she said. "Take his rifle and get back to the front door." Jen propped the piece of wood under the doorknob again, then pointed at where it met the floor. "We need a hole there now."

Chris nodded and raised the axe over his head. Jen stepped back, and Chris swung, creating a crack in the linoleum. With a few more deft strokes, there was a nice groove. Jen propped the piece of wood again, and it fit perfectly. The banging at the bathroom door continued.

Jen bent forward and propped her hands on her knees. Chris stepped back and let out a long breath. "They're not getting through there. It would take more of them than can fit in the bathroom."

Jen straightened and wiped her brow. "I'm exhausted. I think the adrenaline's beginning to wear off."

Chris pointed to a kitchen area. "Why don't you go get some coffee and sit for a bit. We're pretty secure right now."

"I might just do that." Jen walked over to the kitchen, where a pot of oily looking coffee sat. She poured a cup, leaned against the counter, and drank, the bitter liquid burning down her throat. The damn stuff must've been sitting there for hours.

Devin wandered over and stood next to her. She made a face and pointed to her cup. "Crappy, but it's the only game in town. Want a cup?"

Devin shook his head.

"Are all your expeditions this fun-filled?" Jen asked.

Devin gave her a weary smile. "Guess I saved the best for last." He took Jen's hand. "I know I was a shitty father, and I'm sorry."

Jen waved him off. "Not the time. We'll talk once we get out of here."

"That's the first thing we'll do when we get back to Anchorage," Devin said.

Raymond strode up to them. "I'm not sure this place will hold when those sailors get here, but I've got a plan."

"I'm all ears." Devin stood. "Is there anywhere more secure in the village?"

"I'm not talking about here. Wainwright."

Jen had been taking a drink and almost spit up the coffee. "Are you crazy? That's what we tried to do, and we lost Hal. Those things were as thick as flies out there."

"What's going on?" Chris asked as he joined the group.

"Your uncle is contemplating suicide," Jen said. "He wants to go to Wainwright." She crossed her arms. "What is it about that place? Everyone wants to go, but no one seems to get there."

Raymond frowned. "I've got a plan, and I've got twenty-seven other villagers willing to go."

"What's the plan?" Devin folded his arms.

Raymond took a deep breath and exhaled. "Since there are hundreds of the sailors coming from the south, we head east for about five miles, then swing out around them. They won't even know we're there. They'll keep coming here and we'll slip away."

Jen frowned. Sounded like a decent plan, but she remembered Hal's screams. She didn't want to be caught by the zombies out on the dark tundra. "Why not just wait here, and keep that as plan B if the community center looks like it'll be overrun?"

"By the time that happens," Raymond said, "it'll be too late. There'll be too many zombies for us to fight through to get out."

"You've got a point there," Jen said.

"So are you with me?" Raymond asked.

Jen looked at Devin. "What do you think?"

Devin frowned. "It's suicide." A loud bang came from the front door. It rattled.

Raymond crossed his arms. "It's suicide to stay. I learned in the corps that you have to adapt to the situation. This isn't the first solution I'd pick if we had other options, but we don't."

"This will be the first place rescue teams will look," Devin said.

"So you're staying?" Raymond asked.

Devin nodded.

Jen's heart fluttered. She liked Raymond's plan better, but she'd stick with Devin. "Then I'm staying."

Raymond looked at Chris. "And you?"

Chris stepped next to his uncle. "Gotta stick with family." He and Jen locked eyes for a moment. They weren't so different.

Raymond called out. "Clear the front door. We're going through."

He strode to the door, and other members of his group stood behind him, their faces somber.

Devin took Jen's arm and tugged. "We don't want to be too close."

She shook her head. "We should at least help them get clear of the building. Plus we'll need to make sure the door gets secured after they leave." She jogged toward the group at the front door.

Raymond locked eyes with Jen for a second, his jaw set. "On the count of three."

"One." He removed the iron bar from the door.

"Two." He unlocked the deadbolt.

"Three!"

The group slammed into the door, and it opened

outward a couple of feet. The growls and snapping jaws grew louder, and a bloody, flesh-eaten hand grabbed for Raymond. He pointed his shotgun into the opening and fired.

"Again. Harder!" Raymond yelled. "Now."

The group pushed again, with help from villagers that were staying. The door opened halfway and the group pushed outside, guns booming and blunt weapons smashing into skulls. They moved through the zombies inches at a time, but they made progress.

Jen aimed at several zombies but couldn't get a clear shot.

Raymond's head rose above all, and fire spit from his shotgun barrel. The zombies swarmed them, but they slashed their way through the mob. Soon, all that could be seen was Raymond's head as the zombies encircled the group, but still they trudged their way forward. Jen's pulse raced. *They're going to make it.*

A cry of alarm turned Jen's attention to several zombies that had noticed the open community center door and all the fresh meat behind it.

A teenage zombie with a mangled arm rushed Devin, who wrestled him to the ground. Holding the creature down with one arm, he swung the pipe over his head and struck the zombie's forehead. Its head split and it went motionless.

Jen lined up her sights on one of the remaining zombies and shot it in the bridge of its nose. Another couple of quick shots and the remaining threat was gone.

A deafening boom came from behind Jen, and half of a zombie's head exploded in a gore-infused mist.

Jen ducked and looked behind her. Griffin stood, both hands holding the .357, a curl of smoke floating up from the end of the barrel. He smiled at Jen. "Not bad, huh?"

Asshole.

The group of escaping villagers made it across the street, almost through the zombie horde.

A scream came from the group, followed by a cacophony of screeches rising from the other side of the melee. Raymond looked back at the community center, his face slack and eyes wide. "Sailors," he mouthed.

A wave of the infected washed over the group. Several mottled hands grabbed Raymond's head and pulled him from sight.

12

Jen reloaded and fired several rounds, making kill shots with most of them. "We need to open a hole on this side so they can come back."

Devin and several villagers rushed the back of the zombie horde, felling the creatures with deft blows to the head. The zombies were so intent on attacking Raymond's group, they mostly ignored Devin and the other villagers. And the few that tried to attack them were quickly dropped by one of Jen's bullets.

The wall of undead villagers broke down, and two of Raymond's group stumbled toward the community center. One, a young woman, had a gaping bite wound on her cheek. *God forgive me.* Jen sent a well-placed shot into the infected woman's forehead and she collapsed.

Jen kept the gun aimed at the other survivor, a man. His head down, he fell to his knees and looked up at her. *Chris.*

"Help Uncle Raymond," he breathed.

The zombie horde had turned their full attention to Devin and the villagers. "Fall back," Devin yelled as the man to his right was yanked into the mass of undead and disappeared.

Jen and Devin each took one of Chris's arms and half dragged him through the door. The last of the villagers ran into the building. Devin let go of Chris and slammed the door, but not before a withered hand shot through and prevented it from closing all the way.

Devin strained to keep the door from being pried open. "Need help here."

Two villagers rushed to join him, but five more hands shoved through the small opening, grasping for victims. One man holding the door screamed. A toddler had crawled through and bit his ankle. The man released the door and stumbled backward before tripping over a table and falling on his back. His head bounced off the floor and he lay still. The toddler crawled to the unconscious man and chewed on his thigh.

The door opened farther as another zombie pushed halfway through, almost grabbing Devin's arm. Jen lowered Chris onto a chair and pulled her gun back out, shooting the zombie. It went limp and wedged in the doorway, keeping Devin and the villagers from getting the door closed.

She looked around. Where the hell was Griffin?

Chris stood, shaking his head as if to clear it. "We need to get out of here. Those things are coming in whether we want them to or not." He cupped his hands to his mouth. "Devin, we've got to go."

Devin wrestled with a bearded seaman who kept trying to grab him by the neck.

"Devin," Chris shouted again, but he still didn't turn.

Jen took a few steps toward the door and bellowed, "Devin."

Devin looked back.

"Let's go."

A gnarled hand shot out from the doorway and grabbed a villager, who hacked at the arm with a knife. Two zombies climbed over their dead comrade in the doorway, and the rest of the villagers trying to shut the door fled. Devin pushed away an outstretched hand and ran to Jen and Chris. "What do we do now?"

Chris jerked a thumb over his shoulder. "All the zombies have been attracted to the front door, so we'll go out the back."

The front door was ripped off its hinges, and zombies, both fresh villagers and ancient seamen, rushed into the community center. Jen grabbed Devin by the arm and ran to the back of the building. Screams of anguish followed.

Jen stopped short. Damn door was chained and locked. "Are you freaking kidding me?"

Devin pulled on the chains. "Who has the key?"

Chris came to a sliding stop. "Uncle Raymond does." He hefted the fire axe. "But I have the master key. Stand back."

Chris swung the axe and it bounced off the lock. "Shit."

Two seamen zombies stumbled toward them. Devin took one out with a blow to the head, and Jen dropped the other with a bullet.

Chris hacked at the lock again. The damn thing dented, but didn't open.

Several of the villagers who had been attacked minutes before rose from the floor, their yellow eyes searching for a meal.

Jen squared off next to her father. "Chris, you better get that open now or we're the main course in an all-you-can-eat zombie buffet."

One of the zombie villagers sprinted toward them, and

Jen raised the pistol. Devin stepped in front of her. "Save the bullets."

He timed his swing early and missed the zombie, who sprung on him, driving him to the floor.

A loud *clank* and a whoosh of fresh air came from behind Jen.

Devin held the zombie's snapping jaws inches away from his neck. "Need some help here."

Jen lined up the pistol on the zombie, but it was too close to her father.

Several zombie sailors stumbled toward them. *I have to take the shot.* Her finger pressed against the trigger, she followed the zombie's head as it snapped its jaws at her dad. If she could time it when its head was the furthest away from her father—

The axe sliced down and embedded in the zombie's skull with a thud. It fell to the side. Chris yanked the axe free, and Jen pulled Devin to his feet. "Out the door. Now."

The sailors were almost on them, with villagers pushing them from behind. The villagers would've already feasted on them if the slower sailors hadn't been in the way.

Jen and Devin stumbled outside, and Chris slammed the door closed. He put his back against it and held it shut.

"Where do we go?" Jen asked. "And if you say Wainwright, I'm kicking you in the nuts."

The door shuddered, but Chris held it closed. No way he'd be able to keep that up for long. Jen braced herself against the door and Devin joined them.

"We need to find somewhere to hide until the plane comes," Chris said.

Devin's eyebrows rose. "You think it's really coming?"

"I don't know, but it's our best hope."

Jen grunted as the door inched out. "What's the big building on the other side of the village?"

Chris pushed just as the door started to open. It closed again. "The school? Not a bad idea, but we'd have to go through those things out front to get there."

The door opened a few more inches. Jen strained to help keep it back. "We need to go somewhere now." The lights of the science trailers caught her eye. "Up there."

Devin glanced over his shoulder. "Perfect. We can see the whole village from there, then map a path to the school."

The door pushed out again. Jen gritted her teeth and gave it all she had, but it wouldn't budge. Arms shot out from the foot-wide opening, and she slid over to avoid them. "Devin," she yelled. "Get up the hill."

"But what about you two?"

"We'll follow, but you need a head start. Go!"

Devin ran.

"Take the right side," Chris called out.

Jen gasped. The door opened another couple of inches.

"These things will only follow us up the hill," Chris said.

Jen looked for her father and found him disappearing behind a building next to the hill. "The slower ones are in front. If we let the door open quickly, maybe they'll fall and stack up. It could slow the fast ones in the rear."

Chris nodded. "If we don't go straight toward the hill, we might throw them off. Let them see us go in a different direction, then circle back around."

Jen grunted. Her muscles burned. If they didn't go soon, she might not have the strength to run. "I'll follow you. On three. One, two, three."

They let the door go, and Chris dashed off to a house on the right. Jen sprinted after him, a chorus of screeches chasing her. She glanced over her shoulder. The plan had mostly worked. A half dozen of the slower zombies lay in the doorway, blocking the others. But two dead villagers pushed their way over the fallen sailors and chased after them. One of them was an overweight middle-aged man. He ran at no more than a jog. The other, a twenty-something woman in an I Heart Alaska T-shirt, had a chunk missing from her thigh. She limped and was only slightly faster than the man.

Twenty feet ahead, Chris disappeared around a corner. Jen followed a few seconds later and nearly ran into a bare-chested man in bloody jeans. He growled at her and gave chase. Chris was still ahead of her, but stopped and cocked the axe back. Jen dove for the ground at his feet as he swung. She rolled and came up on her knees. The zombie lay a few feet away, its head removed.

"I owe you one," she said.

"Let's hope you don't have to pay me back." Chris grabbed Jen's hand and pulled her up. She followed him in a zigzag pattern between the houses, finally coming to the bottom of the hill, below the science trailers.

Chris pointed up the slope. "There." Devin had made it halfway to the ledge the trailers sat on.

They climbed the slick grassy hill, slipping twice, but caught up with Devin. When he saw them, he sat, his lungs heaving. "Need a rest."

Jen took one arm. "Not here. We're too visible."

Chris took Devin's other arm, and they hauled him to his feet. Half carrying Devin, they climbed the rest of the way to the trailers.

Jen glanced down at the village. Dozens of zombies milled around outside the community center, while groups of two and three wandered between houses. A gunshot and a man's yell came from somewhere to her right, and the group outside the community center screeched as one and ran, stumbled, and crawled toward the sound.

Familiar growling came from below her. Two zombies lurched out of the shadows of a house, their eyes fixed on her. *Looks like they don't all leave when there's a swarm.*

"We're gonna have company," she said. "But they're the slow sailors, so it'll take them a while to get up here."

Devin and Chris joined her, peering down the hill. "Shit," Chris said. He pointed to the slope off to their left. Several figures scaled it like spiders on a web.

Jen's heart hammered. "Villagers."

A screech came from her left and a sailor shambled toward them. Chris lifted his axe. "I've got this one."

Another zombie joined the sailor. Its yellow eyes locked on Jen.

He looks familiar.

Jen's eyes grew wide. "Pete."

13

Chris swung his axe wildly at Zombie Pete and missed, nearly slicing into Jen's arm on the follow-through. She jumped back. "Hey!"

Devin gave Pete a glancing blow in the shoulder with the pipe. It was enough to knock him off course as Jen dodged to the side. Pete hit the ground and recovered, ready to spring.

The sailor rushed Chris, who sidestepped him and brought the axe blade down. He missed the sailor's head, but cleaved his remaining arm from his body.

Pete screeched, then leapt at Jen. She ducked and Pete sailed over her, his head meeting a well-timed swing from Devin. Pete's skull caved in just above his temple and he landed in the mud, sprawled and unmoving.

Chris charged the sailor and didn't miss as he drove the axe blade into its forehead, downing the creature. He propped the axe against the trailer and wiped the sweat from his brow. "That's becoming a workout. Why didn't you just shoot Pete?"

Jen straightened and cracked her neck. "I'm a great shot, but shooting leaping zombies in the head isn't something I've practiced." She pulled the magazine from the pistol and checked the rounds. Two in the magazine and one in the chamber. "Almost out of ammo. No use wasting it."

"Smart." Chris picked up the axe.

Devin smacked the pipe against his palm. "How do we get to the school from here?"

Snarls sounded closer from below. Jen tried to picture the village as she saw it when they landed.

Of course. "What if we go out and around the village."

Chris smiled. "Brilliant. We can follow this hill to the northern side of the village, then circle around and approach the school from the tundra."

Zombie screeches echoed from the village below. "No time to waste." Chris slung the axe over his shoulder and strode toward the north end of the hill.

Jen pulled Devin's arm. "Come on. No time to think about it." She let him go ahead of her while she kept watch from behind.

Chris kept from the edge of the flat part of the hill, but soon came to its end at a steep slope. "We'll have to go up to the runway to go the rest of the way. The slope at that side is more gradual."

"But if we go higher up the hill," Devin said, "we'll be out in the open and won't have that lip to hide us from the village."

Jen ran her fingers through her hair. "The zombies won't be able to get up the slope. And they're too stupid to think of going around."

"Right," Chris said. He pulled the axe off his shoulder and started climbing, using the axe like a walking stick.

Jen looked at Devin and gestured up the slope. "Age before beauty."

A slight grin broke out on his face for a moment, then he trudged up the hill after Chris.

Jen had made it halfway up when activity below caught her attention. She glanced down. Several dozen zombies stood at the base of the hill, attempting to climb it. One would get several feet up the steep slope, then slip and fall, knocking over the others.

More zombies gathered at the same spot, making it more difficult for them.

We work great as bait. If we could just get them to stay there, we'd have free rein of the village. She reached the runway. Chris and Devin stood on the edge. "Looks like we've attracted some attention," Chris said.

"How many do you think there are?" Devin asked.

Chris shrugged. "Two hundred and seventy-one souls in Point Wallace. If we assume most of them have been taken, that'd be at least two hundred. Add a couple hundred sailors and what's down there looking at us isn't a lot of what's out there."

Jen walked across the runway and looked out over the Chukchi. The wind shot off it, blowing small raindrops into her face like tiny needles. Devin stopped next to her.

Chris ran over. "A small horde has made it to the trailer. Won't be long before they're here."

Jen swept hair out of her eyes and the wind blew it back over. "After you."

Chris hurried toward the northern end of the runway. He stopped at the edge, and Jen and Devin caught up with him.

"It's a gradual slope, but it's rocky and easy to slip on the small stones that litter it, so be careful." He started down, using the axe to help him balance.

"Why don't you go next?" Devin asked.

"I've got the gun. I can cover you guys from behind."

Devin frowned. "But who's going to cover you?"

A screech came from behind, and Jen glanced over her shoulder. "Shit. A couple of them are already here. We go together."

She grabbed Devin's arm and they stepped onto the slope. Jen slipped, but righted herself by holding onto him.

Chris had made it halfway down and his path looked to be clear. Jen and Devin hurried to catch up. Jen kept her eyes on the ground in front of them, trying to avoid any rocks. *Freaking impossible.*

They'd reached the halfway point when a zombie screech came from the top of the slope. Echoed by three more, it sent a shock down Jen's spine. Four villagers stood at the top of the slope. One sprinted toward them and the others followed a second later.

Devin stopped. "We won't beat them to the bottom."

Tight-lipped, Jen turned to face the oncoming horrors. "Then we make a stand here."

14

Jen and Devin stood shoulder to shoulder as the four zombies barreled toward them. A teenage girl was in the lead, with the others spread out behind her.

Jen wiped raindrops from her eyes and glanced down the hill. Chris had just reached the bottom.

She aimed her gun at the lead zombie, trying to keep the sight on its head. "It's moving too damn fast and its head keeps bobbing."

Devin tightened his grip on the pipe. "I've got this."

"The others aren't far behind," Jen said. "If we don't take them out quick as each one arrives, we could end up fighting all four at once."

Can't let Devin take them all himself.

Jen went down on one knee and aimed the gun at the lead zombie. Sure enough, its midsection bobbed as it bounded, but there was always a portion of it in her sight.

She took a deep breath, let half of it out, held it, and squeezed the trigger. The gun's recoil pushed it into her hand and the shot hit the zombie just under the ribcage.

It lost its footing and fell, growling and tumbling toward them. Jen tugged on Devin's arm. "Get out of the way."

She and Devin scooted aside and the zombie rolled by. Chris stood at the base of the hill, his axe drawn back.

"One down, three to go," Jen said. She lined up her sights on the next zombie. The round missed its midsection and hit it in the leg. It fell, but didn't roll. The two remaining zombies streaked past it.

"Shit," Jen said. "We'll still have to take care of three."

The two lead zombies bore down on them.

Devin dug his feet in and crouched. "I'll just have to get the rest. You should get down the slope with Chris."

"Always got to play superman, don't you?" Jen said. "I'm not going anywhere."

The zombie she'd shot in the leg had regained its feet and limped toward them, then its leg folded and it fell to the ground.

"Holy shit," Jen said. "I think the bullet shattered its bone."

She took aim at one of the lead zombies. "You take the one on the left. I'll at least slow down the one on the right. Give you some breathing room."

Devin licked his lips. "All right."

Sweat beaded on her forehead.

Twenty yards out. She lined up the sights on its chest.

Fifteen. Wounding it won't work. It'll be too close. I have to make a kill shot.

Ten yards. Jen lined up the sights on the creature's nose. Its head bobbed up and down. Holding her breath, she waited until its eyes disappeared below her sights and squeezed.

The bullet entered the zombie's head between the

bridge of its nose and an eye. The creature dropped, the momentum rolling it down the hill straight at Jen. It took out her feet and she slammed to the ground, dozens of sharp rocks pressing into her back like ground glass. She gasped.

Devin grunted, and the hollow ringing sound of the pipe reverberated over Jen. A body hit the ground, rolled a few feet past her, and lay still, its stench slapping Jen in the face.

She groaned and pushed herself up into a sitting position. Devin reached down and pulled her to her feet. "I'm going to feel this one for a while," she said.

"Thanks to you," Devin said, "we made it out of this in one piece."

Chris called out. "No time to stand around. More can come at any time."

He stood over the first zombie. Its body lay at his feet and he yanked the pointed end of the axe from its head.

Jen and Devin stumbled down the rest of the slope, stopping at the base. Jen stretched her back. "Glad to get on flat ground again."

"No time to rest," Chris said. "Follow me." He and Devin hurried off. Jen looked back up the slope, then jogged to catch up.

They walked a couple hundred yards into the tundra before Chris stopped. "There's no telling if some of those sailors are still out here, so keep your eyes open."

Jen hadn't thought of that. She couldn't help but glance over her shoulder every thirty seconds or so.

The rain and wind picked up as Devin led them in an arc around the village, which was still in view. Screeches reached them several times, and a few shadows flitted around between the lights of the houses.

Chris stopped. "The school is straight in front of us, at the edge of town. It'll be the first thing we reach."

Jen swallowed. "Don't get me wrong, I'm glad we're not going into the middle of the village again, but those things can pop out anywhere."

"Even out here," Devin said.

Thanks for the warm and fuzzy thought. "Then what are we waiting for?"

The three of them walked toward the village.

A woman's shriek followed by the boom of a shotgun came from somewhere deep in the village. Answering screeches replied immediately.

"I think we should pick up the pace," Jen said. "Get in there while they're distracted."

"Agreed," Devin said.

They broke into a jog, feet splashing in pools of water collecting on the tundra. As they closed in on the school, screeches from the village became louder. The school loomed, a single-story solid looking structure. The side they approached had a number of windows, but no doors. *It could be in any small town in America and look like it belonged there.*

"There are two main double doors," Chris said. "One on each end."

"What if they're locked?" Devin asked.

Chris shook his head. "I've never seen them locked. This is a small village and it's hard to get away with anything, so the school's always been safe."

Screeching echoed from beyond the school on their left. They reached the school and Jen nodded toward the other end of the building. "I guess we take door number two."

Chris led them to the corner and peered around it. "Nothing moving."

Jen strode past him. "Then let's get the hell in there." She scooted to the double doors and pulled on a handle.

Locked.

"Shit."

15

Chris tried the other handle. It didn't move. "I've never seen this before."

Jen pressed her face against the window, peering past the thin crisscrossed wires in it. Shading her eyes, she gazed down a hallway. Nothing moved.

"Guess we'll have to go to the other door after all," Devin said. Tight-lipped, Chris pushed past them and around the building. Jen made sure Devin kept up, and hurried after Chris.

When they reached the other end, Devin put a hand up and they stopped. Jen cocked her head but heard nothing.

"Thought I heard a screech," Devin said.

Chris glanced around the corner and pulled back. He waved the other two over and whispered, "Three of them down the road, four buildings on the right. They're just wandering around."

"What should we do?" Devin asked.

Jen propped her hands on her hips. "We can't stay out here all night. We should try the doors."

"And what if they're locked and those zombies see us?" Devin asked.

"What other choice do we have?" Jen replied. "Besides, there's only three. We can take them."

Chris shrugged. "I agree—"

Jen ducked around the corner on the balls of her feet and crept to the doors. Glancing over her shoulder, she padded to the first door and pulled on the handle.

It didn't move.

Fuck.

She took a deep breath and pulled on the other door handle. Locked. Sweat broke out on her forehead and her heart kicked into overdrive.

A screech sounded behind her. She spun. One of the zombies had detected her, and the other zeroed in on her as well.

Devin and Chris rushed to her with questioning eyes. She shook her head. "Both locked."

More screeches came from somewhere ahead, no farther than a couple of buildings away. Answering calls came from all around them.

"There are more than three," Devin said. "We need to get out of here. Head back into the tundra."

More calls rolled in from the tundra. *What the hell?*

Chris looked the way they'd come. "There's at least two dozen sailors heading straight for us. They're not real close and they're not real fast, but they've cut us off that way."

"The school's our only chance," Jen said. "If the doors are locked then someone must be inside."

The three zombies down the road closed in.

Jen peered into the school. A corridor ran from the locked doors to the other exit fifty yards away. A second corridor split off halfway between them on the right.

Jen kicked the door. "Help. Let us in," she yelled.

Chris joined her, banging his fist on the window. Jen shook the handle and rattled the door in its frame. "Open up. They're coming."

"I need some help with the zombies," Devin said. He stood in a defensive stance, the pipe cocked over a shoulder.

Chris hefted his axe and joined him.

Jen glanced their way. The three zombies were almost on them and another dozen appeared in the distance.

A head stuck out from the side hallway and looked at her. *Griffin.* Jen's heart leapt and she banged her open palm on the window, the force sending a shock up her arm. "Open the doors!"

Griffin's head pulled back. *What the fuck?*

Jen turned to the others just as the three zombies reached them. Devin swung his pipe in a perfect golfing drive shot, slamming one zombie in the chin and knocking it backward. Another fell to Chris's blade. The third slammed into Devin and drove him to the ground. Jen grabbed it by the neck and pulled, but the damn thing was strong and only interested in Devin.

Devin struggled to keep it away from his face.

"Get back," Chris said. Jen stepped away and the axe came down in an arc, splitting the back half of the zombie's skull.

Jen helped Devin up. "Not done yet," Chris said.

Jen looked down the street. The dozen zombies had turned into two dozen. *Too many to handle.*

She pressed her face to the door. A woman's head peeked out from the middle corridor. "Open the door," Jen yelled.

The lady didn't move.

"Chris," Jen said, "there's a woman in here but she's just standing there."

Chris looked in the window. "Miss Janine," he yelled. "It's Chris. Chris Nageak. Open the door, please."

The lady made a few tentative steps into the hallway. She was a small thing, not much taller than five feet, and she moved like a scared mouse.

"Miss Janine," Chris yelled. "We don't have much time. Please. Open the door now."

The lady made a few more tentative steps.

"I'm going to die if you don't open the door now," Chris yelled.

"I need some help here," Devin said. Chris slammed his open fist on the frame, then joined Devin.

Miss Janine was almost at the door. Jen didn't want to break eye contact with her. "Just push the bar and open the door. We'll get in, but none of them will. We can help you. We can help each other."

"Get ready for incoming," Devin said. "Forget the door, Jen. We need your help."

The growling and sounds of rushing footsteps were almost upon them. Jen lined up one of the leading zombies in her sights. She squeezed the trigger.

The gun clicked empty.

16

A *clunk* came from behind Jen and something pressed into her back. She reached out as she turned, and Miss Janine disappeared into the side hallway. But Jen's arm held the door open.

She pulled it wider. "Get in!"

The wave of zombies was only yards away. Devin hurried through the door, but Chris didn't move.

"Chris," Jen yelled. "What the hell are you doing?"

He seemed in a trance as the horde bore down on him. Jen stretched out, grabbed his collar, and yanked him through the door. She pulled it closed and fell to the floor as the horde reached the building.

They pounded on the doors and windows, their drool mixed with blood and gore running down the pane.

Chris continued to stare at the horde, his mouth hanging open.

Jen picked herself up gingerly, her shoulder and hip throbbing. "What's wrong with you? You almost got yourself killed."

Chris pointed at the window. His lips moved, but nothing came out. Jen spun.

Towering over the zombie faces pressed to the window was Raymond.

He pushed his way to the front. Chunks of flesh were missing from both his arms and legs, and his eyes had a hunger she'd never seen in another human. He slobbered and reached out to grab her, but was denied. He screeched, and it went right through Jen.

"I'm sorry," she said.

"Uncle." Chris rushed to the window. Raymond took his eyes off Jen and looked at his nephew as if he were a thick, juicy steak.

A pang of sympathy rose in Jen's chest. She put a hand on Chris's shoulder. "It's not him anymore."

He shrugged her off. Devin moved to Chris's other side. "We need to get out of sight. Let these things calm down and disperse."

Chris glared at Devin. "My uncle isn't a thing."

Devin's eyes filled with empathy. "There's no time to be gentle. If more of them come, there's a chance they could break in. So I'm going to be blunt. Your uncle is dead and he's not coming back. What you see out there is a parasite that's taken over his body."

Chris stared at Raymond. "I can't leave him like that. He took care of me all these years, the least I can do is make sure he's at peace."

"Later," Jen said. "Now's not the time. When it is, I'll help you."

Chris studied her for a moment then nodded.

Jen walked him to the side corridor. Miss Janine stood at the other end. Jen strode toward her, and the short woman shrank, but stood her ground. When she reached her, Jen bent over and gave her a hug. "Thank you."

Miss Janine's face turned red. "I couldn't take a chance on them getting in, but I also couldn't let them kill you." Her voice came out soft, almost like a whisper.

Chris hugged her. "You're my hero, Miss Janine."

Devin stood back and nodded at her. "Thanks."

"He told me not to open it," Miss Janine said. "Said it would get the children killed."

"Who told you not to open the door?" Chris asked.

A throat cleared and Griffin stood in a doorway down the hall. "That'd be me. After all, she's got children here. Wouldn't want to put them at risk."

Miss Janine squeezed her hands into fists. "But I opened the door for you."

Jen stormed to Griffin, coming nose to nose. "You pull that kind of shit again and I'll feed you to the zombies myself, one piece at a time."

Griffin put his hands in the air and laughed. "Whoa there, spitfire. No need to be that way."

Jen's pulse pounded in her ears. "Why'd you disappear from the community center and leave us holding the bag?"

Devin put a hand on Jen's shoulder and gently pulled her back from Griffin. "I'd like to know that myself."

Griffin rested a hand on the butt of his holstered revolver. "I saw an opening and took it. Looks like you guys made it out all right."

Chris rushed Griffin, his fist cocked back. Miss Janine stepped in front of him. "I won't put up with any of this. There are children here."

She gestured to the room behind Griffin. "In there. They're already scared, so don't make it worse. Come in and help calm them."

Griffin moved aside and Jen entered the room, catching a whiff of alcohol and body odor as she passed the bootlegger.

The room was a small gym, its only windows near the ceiling. *Good.* Three children, who looked to be between six and ten, sat on a bench, quietly talking among themselves. They stood and bunched together when Jen entered.

"Children," Miss Janine said. "These are friends. They're here to help us."

Chris walked in and the oldest girl's face brightened. "Chris." She ran to him and wrapped her arms around his waist. Chris hugged her back, smiling. "Natalie. I'm so glad to see you're OK."

She took his hand and tears streamed down her face. She sniffled. "Oscar Johnson came in the house and he looked sick. His eyes were yellow and Dad asked him if he needed help."

She wiped her face. "Mom told me to go to my room. That's when Oscar jumped on Dad and they fell to the floor. Then Oscar bit Dad."

Chris knelt next to her. "It's OK, honey. You don't have to think about it anymore."

She shook her head. "And Oscar bit Mom, too. I ran outside. There were other people eating other people. I was so scared. I hid under the Nortons' house and couldn't think of a safe place to go, until I thought of school."

"When I got here," Miss Janine said, "Natalie was hiding in the girl's room. Bobby and Alexei came just after, and that's when I locked the doors."

"And you let in Griffin, too," Chris said.

Griffin sauntered into the gym. Jen eyed him.

"She did," he said. "She's an angel."

"Apparently we wouldn't have gotten in if it hadn't been for this angel," Devin said.

Griffin's eyes narrowed as he glared at Devin.

Jen frowned. *Got to keep my eye on this asshole.*

Devin eased into a chair and wiped his face with his soaked shirt sleeve. "Chris said a plane should be coming in the morning. We can rest here safely until then."

Miss Janine handed a roll of paper towels to Devin. He smiled, ripped a couple of sheets off, and dried his face.

Jen wandered into the hallway. Had Miss Janine checked all the rooms? *Could there be something hiding in here?*

She crept back up the hallway they'd come in and stopped at the intersection with the main corridor. There was still growling and some banging coming from the direction of the door they'd entered, but it had calmed.

She padded back to the room, and Miss Janine was handing out bottles of water. "Would you like one, too?" she asked.

"That would be great." Jen took the offered bottle and drank half of it without stopping. She accidentally let out a belch and the children giggled. Miss Janine gave her a stern look and Jen said, "Excuse me."

Chris leaned his axe against the wall. Jen nodded at it. "You might want to keep that close."

"Why?" Devin asked.

Jen took another swig of water, then put the bottle down. "Miss Janine, have you checked all the rooms in the school to make sure they're empty?"

Miss Janine looked from Jen to Chris then back again. "No. I couldn't leave the children alone."

Jen nodded at Griffin. "And I'll bet Mr. Spineless here hasn't set foot out of this room either."

Griffin gritted his teeth.

Miss Janine shook her head.

Jen cocked her hips to the side and gave Griffin a smirk. "Hoping the kids would protect you?"

The knuckles on his fists turned white, but the bootlegger didn't move. *Just what I thought. Won't do anything when he's outnumbered. What a tool.*

Chris picked up his axe. "I'll check the building." He strode out the door.

Devin sighed and stood, the pipe in his hand. "He shouldn't be doing that alone." He disappeared into the hallway.

Jen gestured to the door, inviting Griffin to leave. "Want to prove me wrong?"

Griffin slid the tomahawk from its sheath. A wicked-looking thing, it was all black except the blade's edge. Griffin handled it easily. "Got this for a bottle of vodka a month ago. Didn't know how handy it would come in."

He gave it a few practice swings, then mimicked Jen's gesture. "Ladies first."

Banging came from down the hallway. "Help," a female voice screamed.

Jen sprinted to the main corridor and glanced at the door they'd come in. There were still a few zombies, and they went bat shit crazy when they saw her, throwing themselves against the door and the windows.

"Open up." A woman stood outside the opposite doorway. "Please," she screamed. She looked behind her, then turned back. "They're coming!"

Griffin caught up with Jen. "Wait. You open that door and the zombies might get in."

"Then you better be ready to fight." Jen sprinted to the door. Four villagers were nearly on the woman.

"Stand to the side," Jen yelled. The woman moved, and

Jen slammed into the bar, throwing the door open. The woman rushed in and disappeared down the corridor. Jen yanked the door to close it, but caught a twenty-something zombie with a shredded arm in the doorway. That gave the other zombies time to attack the opening, keeping Jen from closing the door. She strained to keep it from flying open, but the bar slipped a little at a time through her sweaty fingers. She made an attempt to grab the handle, but the shredded arm zombie snapped at her hand, just missing as Jen yanked it back.

Where are Chris and Devin? She glanced down the hall. *Where the hell did Griffin go?*

Yellow eyes pierced hers, boring into her, through her...almost hypnotic...bared teeth with chunks of meat stuck between them...clacking shut over and over...the death smell washing over Jen as the zombies lunged forward time and again.

She broke eye contact with them and stared at her fingertips turning white as they slipped farther and farther off the bar.

A boom from behind echoed painfully off the walls, and half of the twenty-something zombie's head disintegrated. Startled, Jen fell back and the door flew open.

A zombie leapt onto her and she grabbed it around the neck to keep it away, but her arms had little strength after holding the door closed and they trembled as she struggled. The zombie pushed closer. Jen turned her head and closed her eyes. *This is it.*

A sharp thunk and the zombie went limp. She was able to roll it off her. Devin stood over her, his hand out. She grabbed it and he pulled her up.

Chris and Griffin stood over the zombies, both wiping bloody blades off.

The Awakening

Jen lunged at Griffin. "Where they hell were you?"

Griffin put his hands up and backed away. "Easy there. I just helped save your life."

Jen's legs buckled, and Devin kept her on her feet. "Helped me?" she said. "By running off? Seems that's all you're good for."

"I'm not a big fan of Griffin's," Chris said, "but that's not fair. He came and got us. We didn't hear Marcia's screams from the back of the building."

Jen went cold and shivered so hard she could barely stand. "Adrenaline's leaving your body," Devin said. He led her to the gym and sat her down. Miss Janine handed her a bottle of water and she took a sip.

Devin sat next to her as the others spoke to the new girl. "Griffin shot the first zombie with that big gun of his, then took out the one on top of you with his tomahawk."

Jen swallowed a mouthful of water. "I still don't trust him. He runs too easy."

"It was the right thing to do this time," Devin said. "You were both outnumbered. And we would've never known you needed help."

Jen stood. "Let's go meet the new girl."

She stumbled, but recovered. Devin put an arm around her, steadying her, and they walked over to the others.

Chris gave Marcia a bottle of water. She drank part of it and seemed to be trying to catch her breath.

"Where were you?" Chris asked.

She swallowed. "Home. We need to go back. My dad's there and those creatures are beating on the door. It's only a matter of time before they get in."

"Why didn't he just come with you?" Devin asked.

Chris frowned. "Her father's wheelchair-bound."

Marcia stood. "I've got to go get him."

Chris took her arm. "Sit and rest. I'll get your father." Jen looked at Devin and his gaze met hers. *He's thinking the same thing I am. We're not letting Chris go alone.*

Marcia shifted her position and her pant leg rose for just a moment before it fell. But it was enough time for Jen to see the fresh bite wound on her ankle.

17

Jen nudged Devin and Chris. "Can I talk to you two in the hallway just a second?" She strode out the door without waiting for an answer.

Devin stepped into the hallway with a curious look on his face, while Chris's expression was blank. "What's up?" he asked.

"It's Marcia. She's been bitten."

Chris glanced back into the room, then shook his head. "I didn't see anything."

Jen's heart sank. Chris had lost so many people he knew, even having to put some of them down. She didn't want to give him another one. "Left ankle. It's covered by her pants but they slid up for just a second."

Chris studied her for a minute, then made a beeline for Marcia. Something in his expression must have alarmed her, because she leaned away from him. "What's wrong?"

Chris crossed his arms. "Lift your pant legs."

Marcia slid down the bench a few inches. "What are you talking about?"

Jen and Devin took positions on either side of Chris. "Your ankle," Jen said. "You've been bitten."

"Son of a bitch." Griffin drew his revolver and stepped away from Marcia.

Miss Janine gasped. "Children, come to me."

Marcia's face fell and tears welled in her eyes. "Please don't kill me," she sobbed.

Jen's gut ached. She could only imagine how Chris felt.

Chris glanced at his axe propped against the wall, then at Jen. "If we lock her in a classroom and leave her until she turns, then she won't feel a thing when we have to..."

Devin frowned. "It's a big risk."

"You ain't shitting," Griffin said. "This is why I didn't want to let anyone in."

Miss Janine looked at Chris. "Why don't we just let her go outside?"

"Miss Janine," Jen said, "please take the children to another room."

Miss Janine herded the children out. Devin looked at Jen, his eyes searching hers. "What do you want to do?"

Jen stepped in front of Griffin and put her hand out. "I'll do it."

Griffin shrugged and handed her the .357 Magnum. The damn thing weighed a ton.

She turned to Marcia and the woman wailed. "You can't be serious," Chris said.

Jen pointed the gun at Marcia's head and Chris grabbed her wrist, pulling her arm up. "No more," he said. "There's been enough killing."

Jen's gaze seared his. "She's going to change and it's going to be soon. If we let her go, she's one more zombie between us and the plane. Maybe even the one zombie that infects another one of your neighbors."

Chris stared at her, then blinked. His eyes lowered to the floor and he gave a slight nod. Devin turned away and Griffin crossed his arms, watching her with a curious expression on his face.

Marcia lay on the floor in the fetal position, sobs racking her body. Her pant leg had pulled up again and the bite mark was there for all to see. The skin around it had turned black and the veins leading from it were discolored.

Jen aimed at Marcia's head. Her hands shook so much she struggled to keep the gun steady. Swallowing, she said, "We'll get your father and bring him back here." She took a deep breath and squeezed the trigger, the report of the blast deafening as it echoed off the close walls. The sweet aroma of burnt gunpowder invaded her nostrils and caused her to cough.

Marcia lay still, a bloody hole in the side of her skull and blood pooling around her head.

Devin cleared his throat. "I'll clean up. You go sit."

Jen walked slowly to the other side of the room and sat on a bench, facing the wall. She hadn't signed up to make those kinds of decisions. *But who the hell else is going to make them?*

Griffin put his hand over the revolver. "Someone had to do it."

Jen released the gun and stared at the floor. *Not someone. I had to do it, and I'll be damned for it.*

Her throat tightened. *But I'll make that sacrifice to get us out of here safely.*

Devin's voice broke her from her thoughts. "We should go get Marcia's father."

Jen stood. The body was gone. *How long have I been sitting here?*

Her father's eyes were filled with empathy. His arms

went to encircle her, but he pulled back. *He's as confused about us as I am.*

Jen reached out and pulled him to her.

"I'm sorry I got you into this," he said.

She broke the embrace and wiped her eyes. "Not your fault, Dad."

Devin's eyebrows rose and Jen gave him a weak smile. "That's right. I said Dad, and I meant to."

He nodded, eyes watering. "I've wanted to hear that for a long time."

Chris stood at the doorway, his axe resting on his shoulder. "We should go. No telling when those zombies will break into Marcia's house."

Jen opened a cabinet door. Sports equipment was stored inside, and she rustled through it before picking up an aluminum baseball bat and giving it a few practice swings. "This should work fine."

Miss Janine brought the children back in, but she steered them away from the bloodstained part of the floor with a hole in it.

Griffin walked in wiping his hands together. "Body's wrapped and put in the janitor's closet."

Chris nodded. "Thanks for that."

Griffin shrugged.

Jen approached Chris. "I'm sorry about Marcia."

Chris gave her a fleeting smile. "You wouldn't have had to do that if I'd been strong enough to do it myself."

"When are we going to get the old man?" Griffin asked.

Jen raised an eyebrow. "You're volunteering?"

Griffin licked his lips. "You guys can't keep all the fun to yourselves."

Jen headed to the main corridor. "Then let's go."

She peered around the corner. No zombies in sight at either door. "All clear."

"How can that happen?" Devin asked. "The horde at the community center didn't go away."

"You have to be out of sight and quiet," Griffin said. "That's what made the community center a death trap. Too many people yapping."

Chris chewed his lip. "And the gym is far enough back from these doors that they couldn't hear us. Even the gunshot."

Devin interrupted. "Back to Marcia's father. How far away is his place?"

Chris pointed toward the door Marcia had come in. "Three blocks that way."

Jen strode to the door and pushed it open, keeping it from closing with her foot. Devin and Chris filed out. Griffin looked like he'd rather be anywhere else. "Looks clear," Chris said.

"I'm not seeing anything, either," Jen said.

Devin took a step away from the building. "What are we waiting for?"

Jen eased the door closed. *Locked out again.*

She ran to the first house and ducked underneath. With a height of three feet, the space under the house allowed her to crawl rapidly on her hands and knees.

Growling and banging could be heard somewhere ahead. Chris took the lead while Griffin lingered behind. Chris stopped at the edge of the house, then scurried under the next one. Jen made sure Devin made it before crossing herself.

Griffin ducked down next to her. The banging and growling were closer. "That must be the zombies trying to get into Marcia's father's house," Jen whispered.

Griffin pulled his .357. "Are you nuts?" Jen said. "That'll just bring more of them. Put it away."

Chris pointed to Griffin's sheathed tomahawk. The bootlegger holstered the gun and pulled the tomahawk out.

"How are we going to get in?" Devin asked. "Is there a back door that's clear?"

"One more house until we get there," Chris said. He hustled over and dove under the next house.

The others joined him, and they worked their way to the other side. The damn zombies sounded like they were right on top of them. Jen crawled to the front of the house and looked over. She counted eight of them banging on the front door. She crawled back. "Front's covered pretty good. I don't know how the hell we get past them and then get a guy in a wheelchair out of there."

"Just follow me," Chris said. He ducked under Marcia's father's house and stopped dead in the center. "Watch this."

He reached up and fiddled with something before standing, his upper body disappearing into the house. "Holy shit," Jen said. "An escape door. I never would've guessed."

"In his younger days, Marcia's father was a bootlegger," Griffin said. "Not such a terrible occupation."

Chris pulled himself up and disappeared inside.

"Jen next," Devin said.

Jen hauled herself in. The house was pitch-black. She scooted away from the opening, and Devin climbed in and knelt beside her.

Griffin stuck his head in. "I'll keep the escape route open." He disappeared under the house.

"John," Chris said. "Where are you?"

A flashlight came on, and Chris pointed the beam around a living room and kitchen. It settled on an empty wheelchair lying on its side over by the front door.

"John," Chris whispered harshly. "We're here to take you to safety."

A groan came from behind them, barely audible with all the banging. Chris shined the light on the couch and padded toward it, while Jen crept around to the other side. Chris pointed the beam behind the couch and there an old man lay facedown, struggling to crawl. Chris rushed forward. "Let's get him in his wheelchair." He took one of the man's arms and Jen took the other. Chris held the light out to Devin. "Hold this."

They picked the man up and he struggled. *Damn, he's got some spunk.*

Once John was placed in the wheelchair, Devin shined the flashlight on him. John reared his head back and screeched. He lunged at Jen and fell onto her, knocking her to the floor and trapping her legs with his body. She lost her grip on the bat and it rolled out of reach.

Zombies at the door returned John's screech and doubled their efforts to get in. The door rattled in its frame, then bowed in with a resounding *crack*.

18

Chris wrapped his arms around the old man and pulled him off at the same time Devin grabbed Jen under the arms and yanked her backward.

"Get out," Chris yelled.

Jen scurried to the hole in the floor and dove through. She rolled away from the opening and Devin dropped next to her. Another huge *crack* echoed from the house and footsteps rumbled across the floor.

Chris fell through the opening and onto his stomach. He pushed up to his hands and knees. "Go. They're right behind me."

Jen scrambled back the way they had come, pausing under the house across the road. Devin ran across the gap between the houses, and Chris was hot on his heels. Several zombies were back at the trap door. One dropped to the ground and tried to stand under the house, blocking the others from getting out. *Stupid-ass things.*

"Where the hell's Griffin?" Chris asked.

Jen looked around. Nothing but zombies. She clenched her jaw. *That son of a bitch flaked out on us. Again.*

A screech went up a few houses away. They'd been spotted. Answering calls came from every direction. Jen paused in the middle of the house. "Where the hell do we go?"

"We've got to get back to the school," Chris said.

"Through this?" Devin asked.

Zombie feet rushed by in every direction. They'd be spotted as soon as they came out from under the house. "Maybe we just wait here," Devin said.

Chris pointed behind them. "No time."

The zombies chasing them had finally figured out how to crawl, but they were slow at it. *Can't count on that lasting.*

"How far's Raymond's house?" Jen asked.

"Couple blocks." Chris pointed. "That way. Away from the school."

"Why there?" Devin asked.

The zombies from the house had nearly reached its edge. "The four-wheelers," Jen said. "What better way to outrun these things?"

Chris scrambled forward. "Follow me."

They sprinted across the road and slid underneath another house, leaving several screeching zombies in their wake. Chris didn't stop, and they scrambled to the next house in record time. One more and Chris stopped and pointed. "There it is."

They were catty-cornered from Raymond's, the four-wheelers sitting out front. An old woman, the front of her kuspuk a bloody mess, wandered back and forth on the porch. Two teenage creatures stumbled around several feet from the ATVs.

Jen looked behind her. The pursuing zombies had reached the last house they'd crawled under. Her pulse beat double-time. The undead skittered under it like spiders.

Freaking things have definitely figured out how to move under buildings.

"Zombies coming up on our ass. We have to get on those four-wheelers." She slid out from under the house and raced toward one of the teenage zombies. It noticed her and shrieked. The other one spun, and both sprinted for her. *Shit. Didn't want two at a time.*

"I've got the one on the right," Chris said from behind her.

Jen closed in and reared her bat back. Chris caught up and readied his axe. Five feet away, Jen's zombie leapt at her. Caught off guard, she clumsily swung the bat upward and ducked. She missed the zombie and fell to the ground, but it sailed overhead.

Scrambling to her feet, Jen faced the creature, its yellow eyes burning with hunger. It sprung again, but this time she was ready. She swung and stepped to the side at the same time, the bat connecting with the zombie's ear.

It fell to the ground rolling. When it came to a stop, it pushed itself up, but stumbled while trying to approach her. She ran up to it and bashed it in the nose, blood and bone fragments splattering the front of her shirt. It slumped to the ground.

Devin battled the old woman, while Chris was pulling his axe from the other teenager's skull. Thirty yards down the road in the direction they'd come from, a horde rumbled toward them, big enough to fill the space between houses.

Jen dashed to a four-wheeler, just as Devin took out the old lady. Jumping on, she had a sinking certainty it wouldn't start, but it roared to life as soon as she turned the key. Devin and Chris hopped on their ATVs and started them up.

"Where are we going?" Chris shouted over the engines.

"How long before the supply plane normally comes?" Jen asked.

Chris looked at his watch and held up two fingers. "Couple hours."

The damn horde was only twenty yards away. "Take us to the school," Jen said. "Long way around so we won't be followed."

Chris goosed his accelerator and put the ATV in gear. He shot down the road, heading for the outskirts of the village, with Jen and Devin behind him. They turned a corner, losing sight of the horde, and zoomed out onto the tundra.

Jen wiped moisture from her face. A light rain had started and the wind had eased. *And the clouds are breaking in the distance. Planes should be able to fly soon.*

Chris led them down the path they'd taken before. When they reached the spot where they'd broken off to go to Fear Mountain, he stopped and turned off his engine. Jen and Devin did the same. The silence was oppressive.

"Pretty sad that this is the safest place for us right now," Devin said.

Chris checked his gas level. "And about as far as we go if we don't want to run out of gas out here."

Jen sat back in her seat and closed her eyes for a moment. If she concentrated, she could pretend she was back in Anchorage, hiking in the Chugach Mountains.

The sound of the breeze in my ears.
The stillness.
A screech came from farther out in the tundra.
And fucking zombies trying to eat me.

19

Jen peered out into the dusky tundra. A figure moved. Then another. As her eyes became accustomed to the low light, more and more zombies emerged. "Holy shit. Are the sailors still thawing from the pit?"

"Looks that way." Devin turned on his headlight and aimed it. The beam landed on a couple dozen sailors, their yellow eyes glowing in the light. He swept the beam left, then right.

"There are hundreds more," Chris said.

"So much for being safe." Jen started her engine. "We need to get to the school."

Chris and Devin started up, and the trio headed across the tundra to the far side of the village. Chris started to pull away, so Jen sped up just as a wind gust hit and took her breath away. Bouncing across the uneven ground, she was nearly thrown off her seat. "Slow it down," she yelled. "The sailors don't move that fast."

Chris let back on the throttle, allowing the others to catch up. "We need to get back quick. When these hundreds of sailors show up in town, the place will be thick with them. We won't be able to move."

They rode straight toward the school. Its lights were still on. *Hope Miss Janine and the kids are OK.*

Several yards out, a small horde rushed them from behind a house. Eight strong, six were villagers. The riders had been heading for the far door, and the zombies would soon be between them and their destination.

Chris swung his four-wheeler toward the other door, and Jen and Chris mimicked him. The entrance was clear, but would Miss Janine unlock it in time?

Jen pulled up just as Chris dismounted. She turned off the engine and ran to the door. Chris took a defensive position with his axe and Devin arrived and joined him. "Bang on the door and get Miss Janine out here," he said.

Peering in the window, Jen raised her fist to slam it against the door, but paused. At first everything looked the same. *But that streak of blood at the corridor intersection wasn't there before, and it looks fresh.*

She reached for the door handle and paused. The damn thing wasn't closed all the way. She pulled it open.

Swinging it wide, she said, "Door's open. In now."

Devin and Chris ran in, and Jen pulled the door closed behind her with a *clunk*. The zombies didn't break stride and slammed into the door twenty seconds later.

Chris looked around. "Where's Miss Janine?"

"I don't know. The door was unlocked. In fact, it wasn't even closed all the way."

Devin frowned and peered down the corridor. "I don't like the sound of that."

"Miss Janine," Chris called.

Jen grabbed his arm. "Shh. If something's in here, we don't want to ring the dinner bell."

"We've got to get out of sight of the zombies outside," Devin said, "or they'll do all the ringing for us."

Jen crept down the corridor and stopped at the intersection. The blood streak was wider there. She pointed and whispered, "This wasn't here before."

Chris peeked around the corner. "It comes from down there."

Jen swallowed, a pang rising in her chest. She raised the bat and padded down the hallway to the gym, the noise of the zombies at the door fading.

Chris hugged the opposite wall and Devin stayed at her side. Jen stopped outside of the open gym door. The lights were off inside, cloaking who knew what. She took a deep breath and nearly gagged. It was as if she had stepped into the slaughter room of a busy ranch on a hot summer's day.

Devin covered his nose and Chris made a face. "I may be sick," he said.

Jen waited, but nothing stirred in the gym. *One, two, three.*

She reached in and flipped the light switch, then staggered backward into Devin.

Blood and entrails painted the floor and splattered the walls. The bloody streak started at the benches. Where the kids had been.

Jen turned her head away and staggered into the hallway. Nausea threatened, but she choked down the bile that rose to the back of her throat. *Little kids. They were just little kids.*

Devin rubbed her back.

It took a couple of minutes, but the wave of nausea passed, and tears flooded her eyes. She looked at Devin. "Those kids," she choked out.

Devin pulled her in and encircled her with his arms. "I know."

She laid her head on his shoulder and wept as he soothed her. She'd never had anyone who could console her like that since her mother died. She didn't want to let go.

Can't afford this now. Got to get us out of this first.

She raised her head and pulled back, wiping her eyes. "Sorry. I'm good."

Devin's eyes filled with sympathy. "It's OK to cry, you know."

She gave him a weak smile. "I know, Dad. But I can do that later. Right now we need to concentrate on getting the hell out of here alive."

Jen closed the gym door. Chris leaned against the wall, his face ashen. "The whole village is dead. I'm all that's left."

A bang came from up the corridor. The entrance door.

Were the zombies back? Jen raised the bat, ready to bash in some zombie heads. Devin and Chris closed ranks on her side.

Footsteps clomped down the hall, getting closer.

20

Jen tried to swallow, but her mouth had no spit.

The footsteps still echoed down the hallway. *How the hell long is that walk?*

Griffin appeared at the end of the corridor, his chest heaving. He stumbled toward them.

Jen fought the urge to kick him in the balls.

"You're here," Griffin breathed.

The bootlegger bent forward with his hands on his knees. Chris pushed past Jen. "I'll check that the doors are secure."

Griffin straightened and leaned back against the wall with his eyes closed. His breathing had slowed. "Didn't think I'd make it. That was damn close."

"Where the hell did you go?" Jen asked. "You took off on us again."

His eyes opened and he stared at her, incredulous. "I led them away from you."

Jen scoffed.

"Forgive me," Devin said. "But that sounds like bullshit."

Chris returned. "Doors are good."

Griffin stood. "One of those things was crawling around and spotted me under the house. It made that high-pitched sound of theirs and others came. You guys were still inside and I figured if I joined you in the house then we'd all be trapped."

He crossed his arms. "So I ran and they followed me."

Chris raised his eyebrows and looked at Jen. "He tells a good story, I'll give him that," she said.

Red splotches appeared on the exposed parts of Griffin's face, and he spoke through gritted teeth. "I may be a lot of things, but I'm not a liar. I just went through hell and almost got bitten and now I get interrogated?"

"You didn't get chomped and neither did we," Jen said. "But we can't say the same about Miss Janine and the kids."

"What are you talking about?"

Jen stepped away from the gym door. Griffin looked at her, his head slightly turned and his eyebrows lowered. She nodded at the door. "Go ahead."

Griffin approached the door as if it were about to explode. He grasped the handle lightly and turned it, then looked back at the others. Chris gestured to the door.

Griffin opened it, and the thick odor of slaughter washed into the hallway. The bootlegger stepped back as if it had physically slapped him in the face. He stood still for thirty seconds, then closed the door. He didn't turn back to the others.

"Griffin?" Devin said.

"She saved me." Griffin's voice was thick. "And she was damned and determined to save those children. Babies. They were just babies."

A clattering sound came from the hallway behind them. Griffin whipped around. Devin and Chris went into defensive stances, and Jen's muscles tensed.

She craned her neck, but couldn't see to the end of the hallway where the sound came from. "What's down that way?"

"A couple of classrooms, janitor's closet, and the kitchen and cafeteria," Chris said.

"We better check it out," Devin said.

Chris straightened. "Doesn't have to be a zombie. Maybe Miss Janine and the kids hid down there."

Griffin drew his tomahawk. "Want odds on that?"

"It's possible," Devin said.

"Only one way to find out." Jen crept to the next doorway and scanned the room. "This one's clear."

Chris cleared a room across the hall, while Devin and Griffin took the next one.

The hallway took a bend to the right. Jen stopped there and peeked around the corner. A pair of swinging double doors stood closed twenty feet away. A crash of metal on metal came from behind the door. Jen pulled back and hugged the wall, her heart doing a drum solo. "Sounds like a drawer of forks and knives being dumped on the floor."

"I'm thinking less and less that it's caused by humans," Chris said.

"You think?" Griffin said.

Devin nodded. "Maybe we just block the door? Keep whatever it is in there?"

"Don't think I can stay in here knowing there's something creeping around back there," Chris said.

Jen took a deep breath and let it out slowly. "Then we better get in there and see what's on the menu." She crept around the corner and hugged a wall as she closed in on the kitchen doors. Devin kept up against the other wall, and Chris just plain walked down the middle of the corridor as if he were out on an after-dinner walk. *A stroll with an axe, no less.*

Stopping at the door, Jen looked back to find Griffin right behind her. He smiled and shrugged. *Definitely not counting on him being there when I need it.*

Each door had a two-foot-by-two-foot window at eye level. Jen took up position on one side and peeked in. The kitchen was a landscape of stainless-steel tables and appliances. Metal mixing bowls and utensils were scattered across the tables, range, and floor.

"I see a mess," Jen whispered, "but not what made it."

Devin looked through the other side. "Same here. There are two large stainless-steel doors. One is shut and the other is open about a foot."

Chris pushed a door open a few inches, then entered and moved to the left. Jen and Griffin slipped in behind him. Devin watched their rear.

The kitchen looked as if one of those asshole reality TV chefs had a fit and tossed the whole damn thing. Cabinets were empty and the floor was littered with cooking implements.

Jen nodded at the open stainless steel door. Chris nodded back and took a position on the open side. Devin stepped forward, a solid grip on his pipe, and Griffin held the tomahawk at the ready. Jen grasped the door handle and threw out one finger, then two, then three, and swung the door open.

Jen inched out from behind the door and looked inside a walk-in refrigerator. Boxes were stacked in the back and racks were filled with plastic wrap-covered bowls, large open cans, and condiments.

Damn thing wasn't big enough to hide much, but Jen

stepped in and looked between the boxes and racks. She turned to the others. "Nothing."

Chris held a hand up, then waved for the others to follow him. He tiptoed to a wide opening in the wall with a metal blind pulled down over it. The serving line. Where the lunch ladies ladled out the slop.

Jen stood next to him and listened. It took a minute, but there was no doubt. Someone was eating, and doing it loudly.

Chris pointed to the metal blind, then pointed upwards. Griffin grasped one end and Chris the other. They pulled, but it didn't move. Jen reached over to the bottom of the blind and slid a latch back. They tried again, and the blind slid upward without a sound.

Jen gripped the bat. The blind stopped at the top, but Jen couldn't see the whole cafeteria from her vantage point. Even so, nothing seemed out of place. The chairs were placed upside down on the edges of the tables and the floor looked like it had been washed and swept.

She leaned out the window. The munching sounds drew her attention to the left. There, against the wall, lay Miss Janine, her eyes dull and staring at the ceiling. Four children squatted around her, filling their mouths with bloody meat and organs from her shredded abdomen.

Someone behind her let out a small gasp.

Heat rose in Jen's face and she squeezed the bat. *No more.*

She jumped through the opening and rushed the zombie feast.

21

The kids turned around at the last second, their meals hanging from their mouths.

Swinging the bat underhand, Jen caught Natalie in the jaw. The girl fell back as the other three children jumped to their feet.

Jen's momentum took her past the kids and she skidded into a corner. Natalie rose, her jaw hanging limply and bloody drool spilling from her mouth. The other three children fanned out. Jen stepped out from the corner to give herself more swinging space. *You little shits are going down.*

Devin, Chris, and Griffin came running, and the two boys Miss Janine had cared for with Natalie broke off to meet them. Natalie and another boy Jen didn't recognize closed in on her from opposite sides.

"I'm all dressed up with nowhere to go," Jen said. "So let's dance."

Natalie growled, nothing in her movements indicating anything but a hungry predator.

She can't bite me with a broken jaw. She concentrated on the boy.

Just as sounds of battle came from the middle of the cafeteria, Natalie lunged. Jen feinted, and when the boy attacked a second later, she swung and caught him on the shoulder. *Shit.*

The two zombies backed up, then rushed straight at her as one. Jen raised the bat overhead and stepped into the attack, bringing the weapon down and stepping off to the side. The boy ran past, and the bat came square down on top of Natalie's skull, the crack sudden and brutal. Natalie slumped to the floor and the boy leapt at Jen. Without time for another swing, she rammed the end of the bat into the boy's chest. Knocked back into the corner, he scrambled to his feet and sprung again.

Too damn fast. She barely ducked in time, then stumbled back into the wall. The boy sprung as she turned, but Griffin appeared and buried the tomahawk blade in the back of the kid's head. The momentum slammed the kid into Jen, bouncing her off the wall and to the floor. She pushed the boy's limp body off her.

"Thanks," Jen said.

Griffin wiped off his blade with some napkins and sheathed it. "Do you always do that?"

Panting, Jen asked, "Do what?"

"Just run into the middle of shit." He put a hand out.

She grasped it, and he pulled her up. She smirked. "It's becoming my trademark."

The boy Jen recognized as Bobby lay in a pile in the middle of the cafeteria. Devin and Chris had outmaneuvered Alexei across the room and were closing in from separate sides.

Alexei swatted at Devin, who jumped back. Chris took the opportunity and swung the axe overhead, missing the boy's head, but carving a canyon down his back. The boy stumbled, and Devin bashed his forehead with the pipe. The boy collapsed.

Jen pulled a chair off a table and sat. "Those little buggers were a handful."

Devin stood next to her, bent over with his hands on his knees. "I was wondering who Miss Janine would open the door for after the incident with Marcia." He nodded to the unidentified boy. "Of course, she would for a child."

Chris joined them, giving each a bottle of water. "Found these in the fridge." He unscrewed his bottle and downed half of it. Wiping his mouth on his sleeve, he gave a satisfying belch.

After emptying his bottle, Griffin crushed it and threw it into a trash can ten feet away. He raised his hands in the air. "Score."

Jen took a sip. "I'm getting numb to all this killing. If I would've had to kill these zombie kids at the beginning, I don't think I could've done it. But after I saw them gnawing on Miss Janine in their own version of Mystery Meat Monday, I lost it."

Chris nodded. "I think we're all becoming numb to it, but that's good in a way. It may be the only way we survive."

Devin took a drink, then poured the rest of the water over his head. "I don't know if I can physically do much more of this. I'm not exactly young and in shape." He reached out to Chris. "What time is it? How close are we to the plane coming?"

Chris glanced at his watch. "If it comes at all and if it comes at its normal time, we have about an hour."

Jen walked over to one of the cafeteria's draped windows and pulled back a corner. *Shit.*

Turning back to the others, she said, "Those sailors we met on the tundra? They're about to make port here."

She peeked back out the window and watched as hundreds of zombie sailors lumbered toward the village.

"How are we going to get to the landing strip now?"

22

Jen tipped the water bottle back, letting the last swig empty into her mouth. She swallowed. "The bottom line is we're screwed. The damn runway is on the other side of the village and we're about to have a zombie convention out there."

She picked up her bat and strode to the kitchen door. "We can't wait. Have to make our move before the rest of the undead navy gets here."

Devin rose from his seat. "Why don't we take a boat now that the sky's clearing?"

"Not our best option," Chris said. "Even though the clouds are letting up, it's still windy and the seas will be rough. As a last resort, I'd take it, and we might survive if we kept close to shore. But I still think the plane's our best bet."

"But we don't even know if a plane's coming," Jen snapped. "Even if we can get to the runway, it may be for nothing."

Chris threw the axe over his shoulder. "If the plane doesn't come, then we'll be at the top of the hill and can map a safe path to the boats from there. Just like we did to get to the school."

"I'm not sure about this plan," Griffin said.

"Then you can always stay here," Jen said. Griffin went silent and pursed his lips.

There were no great options, only shitty and shittier ones. How the hell could they get out alive?

Will we get out at all?

The question had bubbled up unbidden from Jen's subconscious. *No time for doubt.* She thrust her jaw out. "We need better weapons, more firearms, and transportation."

"And how do we get that?" Chris asked. "That's a lot to ask for while we try to keep from being eaten."

"We also need a diversion," Jen said. "These things seem to be easy to distract. Why not use that to give us the time to get across the village?"

Devin rubbed his chin. "That's a great idea, but what do we use for a distraction?"

"Something loud," she said. "Maybe something that moves. Lights seem to attract them, too."

Griffin smiled. "Then I'm your man."

"Let me guess," Jen said. "You want to give them booze and let them drink till they pass out."

"It's true I bring in booze," he said, "but it's not all I deal in. I have some top-notch fireworks in my house. You want noise and light? That'll do it."

Jen did a double take. *Damn good idea.* "That's step one. Once the creatures are distracted, where are we going to get weapons and ammo?"

"That's a bit harder," Chris said. "You'd find them in any house, but we don't know which houses have zombies trapped in them."

"What about the community center?" Devin asked.

"There were villagers with guns who dropped them when they were bitten."

"And the doors are knocked down, so no zombies will be trapped there," Jen said.

Griffin pulled his tomahawk out. "Then let's get the hell out of here."

JEN LOOKED out onto the tundra. The sailors shambled along less than a hundred yards away. Between the driving rain and the light fog forming, she had no way to tell how many there were. But what she could see caused her breath to hitch. The damn zombies stretched across the horizon as far as she could see. "We need to move our asses."

"We can't stop once we get going," Griffin said. "So keep up."

Jen gripped her bat. "No crawling around under houses. Too slow."

Griffin took off, catching Jen by surprise. She grabbed Devin's arm and pulled him forward. "Let's go. Keep up, old man." She raced after Griffin, glancing back to make sure Devin and Chris followed.

Griffin had already made it to the next house. He stopped on the side, peering forward and waving for the others to catch up. Jen stopped behind him. "No screeches so far."

Devin and Chris approached from behind. A screech rose from the tundra.

"Me and my big mouth," Jen said.

A symphony of answering screeches roared from the tundra and the village.

"Time to go." Griffin sprinted forward.

Zombies woke up all around, their screeches piercing Jen's ears and sending a jolt down her spine.

When she caught up with Griffin, movement farther in the village caught her eye. A horde of a dozen or so streaked toward them. "We've got to move."

Griffin took off like a runner from a starting block. Jen turned to make sure Devin and Chris followed, but found no sign of them. She ran back into the road and scanned the area.

Another horde, twice as big as the first, stampeded her way.

Jen's breath came in short gasps and her heart threatened to burst. "Dad!"

No answer came.

23

Frozen with indecision, Jen scanned the surrounding area looking for any sign of Devin. *Where the hell'd he go?*

The larger horde was only a house and a half away. She'd have no chance if she didn't leave at once. She cupped her hands and yelled, "I'll be back for you."

She sprinted for Griffin and passed the next road only twenty yards ahead of the first horde. *Holy shit.*

Kicking it into high gear, she neared Griffin. He dashed past the house, then took a left. Jen followed, glancing over her shoulder. The first horde stayed with her and the second, larger one, roared right behind them.

Griffin took an immediate right. They should've been to his house by then. *He's trying to lose them.*

Jen raced around the corner, glancing back at the last second. The horde hadn't come into view yet.

Standing on the porch of unremarkable, weather-beaten house, Griffin held the door open. Jen zoomed through it and Griffin closed it behind him. "Where are the others?"

Jen held back tears. "I don't know. I turned around and they were gone."

Griffin cracked the door open, then eased it closed. He put a finger to his lips. "The zombies are in front," he whispered.

A cacophony of screeches surrounded the house, penetrating the walls and drilling into Jen's head. She didn't dare move. Crouched and ready to spring into action, she stared at Griffin and the door as the stampede of footsteps rumbled by, then faded.

The bootlegger tip toed past her and into a back room. She crept to the room's doorway and watched. An eight-by-eight room practically stuffed with boxes, only one person could fit into it at a time. Griffin lifted a box, then shook his head and tried another.

After three boxes, he pulled one off of a high stack and smiled. He laid it on the floor and pulled the tucked flap open. "Bingo."

Jen didn't know much about fireworks, but recognized that the top package of sparklers wouldn't do them any good. Griffin put that package to the side. He did the same with the next two packages, but paused when he came to the fourth.

"What's that?" Jen asked.

He showed her the package. "M80s. Big-ass firecrackers."

"But don't those just blow up quick, then you have to light another? We'd have to stay in the area to keep those going."

Griffin handed them to her. "Those are the warm-ups."

He pulled another box off the stack, then shook his head and put it to the side. "Booze."

After several more boxes, he stood back with his hands on his hips. "Where the hell did I put it?"

Jen glanced at the door. Her father was still out there. "This is taking too long. What are you looking for?"

Griffin stepped out of the room. "The good stuff. Stuff I was keeping for myself. I hid it somewhere, but can't remember where."

He wandered into the cluttered living room, past the torn, stained couch, and into the kitchen.

Ignoring the piles of dirty dishes in the sink and the trash on the floor, he opened a cabinet and pushed cereal boxes and canned food aside. Shaking his head, he moved to the next cabinet and repeated the process.

Oh, for crying out loud. Jen opened a cabinet and mimicked his actions. *Don't know what the hell I'm looking for.* She found nothing but food.

They met at the last cabinet. Jen stepped back and gestured to it. "This is your treasure hunt."

Griffin checked the bottom shelf, then rifled through the middle one. With a sigh, he pulled a box of bread crackers out then felt behind it. His eyebrows shot up, and he pulled a completely black box out. "This is it."

"This is what?"

"A cake." He flipped it over and read the writing on the back. "A two-minute one."

"We're in the middle of the apocalypse and you want to bake a fucking cake?"

Griffin cleared a spot on the counter and placed the box down. "You really don't know anything about fireworks, do you?"

When she didn't answer, he said, "It's got multiple rockets and shit in it. You light it and it gives you a whole show."

"And it lasts two minutes?"

He nodded. "We toss a few M80s over the next house.

That'll draw them there. Then we head back to the school, light this thing, and book our asses over to the community center. Two minutes is a long time for us to get out of the area."

"One step you missed there," Jen said.

"What's that?"

Jen cleared her throat. "We find Chris and my dad on the way back to the school. We're not leaving them behind."

Griffin let out a long breath. "Look, I don't blame you for not trusting me, but I promise you we'll find them both before we set off the fireworks."

So there's a human being in there after all. Jen clapped him on the shoulder. "We'll all get out of here."

She ripped open the M80 package. "Now let's set off some fireworks."

24

Jen cracked the front door and peeked out. The screeching had stopped. Sensing no movement, she opened it farther and scanned the area. "Clear."

Griffin handed her two M80s. "How's your throw?"

She shrugged. "I throw like a girl."

Griffin made a face.

"I throw like a girl who played softball for years. I can chuck something as small as an M80 far enough."

They stepped onto the porch and faced the house. The rain had died to a steady drizzle. "We need to get these over at least the next house. Don't want to draw the zombies too close to us," Griffin said.

Jen glanced up and down the road. Still clear. "I can do better than that. Mine'll go over the next two houses."

"Good." Griffin removed a box of matches from his pocket.

Jen held an M80 in her throwing hand. "How do you want these spaced? I say we throw one, wait for the explosions, then throw another."

"That'll work. Then we go back into the house and wait for things to calm down before heading to the school."

Jen nodded.

Griffin struck a match against the side of the box and produced a blue-and-yellow flame. Jen lit her wick and threw the M80 high over the house. Two seconds later, Griffin's arced out of sight.

A boom, then another, echoed between the houses. The screeching began, several from close by.

Jen lit her second M80 and flung it, then ducked into the house. Griffin did the same and closed the door behind him, just before two more resounding booms penetrated the walls.

The screeches multiplied and footsteps pounded the ground. *Please let Dad be somewhere safe.*

Griffin opened the refrigerator door. "Want a beer?"

Jen nodded, and Griffin tossed her a can. She opened it and took a swig. No need to whisper with the racket from the zombie stampede outside. "Why?" she asked.

Griffin leaned against the counter and opened his can. "Why what?"

"The bootlegging," Jen said. "Doesn't seem like a good career choice."

Griffin shrugged. "My talents lie in a couple of specific areas." He took a mouthful of beer.

Looking around the kitchen, Jen said, "I'm betting housekeeping isn't in the top ten."

Griffin laughed, spewing beer onto the floor. "Shit."

He coughed and wiped his mouth. "You're a real ball buster." He took another swig and swallowed. "My talents are in flying and selling, and I've taken the best opportunity to do both."

"So you have a plane?" Jen asked.

He shook his head. "Had. Troopers caught me at a dry village with some vodka and my plane was confiscated. So now I just use mail order."

Something bumped into the house and Jen froze, her can of beer almost to her mouth. When no other sound followed, she took another gulp. "Don't get too big of a head, but you're not a dumb guy. Why not get a flying job that pays you?"

Griffin downed the last of the can and placed it on the counter. "I've got a problem with authority figures and I don't play well with others. If you find a company that'll hire me with all that, let me know."

Jen grinned. "Not something I've ever seen on a job description."

Griffin smiled back. He folded his arms and waited.

Things quieted little by little outside until Jen heard nothing else. "Don't think we can wait much longer, or the plane might land before we get there."

A footstep clomped on the porch and Jen's eyes met Griffin's. "Could be my dad," she whispered. She tiptoed toward the door, but Griffin grasped her arm. "Peek out the window first."

Jen crept to the window and pulled back a sliver of the curtain.

Three sailors stumbled around on the porch.

You've got to be freaking kidding me.

25

Jen looked down the road from both sides of the window, then straightened. "What do you see?" Griffin whispered.

"I don't see any others, but I can't see all of the road from this angle." She choked up on the bat. "There could be a horde just out of sight for all I know."

Griffin scratched his beard. "We don't have a choice. No time to wait. We have to take those three out before they can sound the alarm." He frowned. "If there are more out there and they attack, we'll have to fall back in here and figure something out."

Jen nodded. *I've got to get to Dad. What if he's injured?* "I'm with you."

Griffin peeked out the window, then backed away. "Two are just a few feet outside the door. It's the third one that worries me. It's halfway across the porch."

"You go for that one," Jen said. "I'll take care of the other two."

"How's that going to work?"

Jen licked her lips. "You run between the first two. Ignore them and get the other one. You'll have to be fast."

"And you?"

"I'll take care of mine. Don't you worry."

Griffin laid the cake package on the couch. "OK. Let's do it."

They huddled at the door and Griffin turned the knob slowly. He nodded, then breathed, "Three, two, one."

He burst out the door and rammed between the two closest sailors. Jen stepped out and swung at the head of one of them, hitting it square in the back of the head. It dropped, and Jen reared back while the other sailor turned on her, its eyes glittering. It tilted its head back and Jen jerked the bat around and smashed its nose. Teeth scattered on the porch.

Griffin rushed the other sailor. They'd lucked out; it had been facing away from them. But it heard him coming and spun to meet the threat. *Damn. A fast sailor zombie? What the hell?*

It leapt at Griffin, who jumped to the side and was able to take a chunk from its chest with a swing of the tomahawk.

Jen's remaining sailor stumbled backward, but managed to keep its feet. It tilted its head back, but all that came out was a weak whistling sound. Jen cocked the bat back and let it fly, crushing the sailor's skull at the temple. It fell to the porch.

Griffin's sailor pulled itself to its knees. Grunting, Griffin brought the tomahawk overhead and planted the pointed end into the top of the zombie's head. It slumped and lay still.

Jen backed to the door, her head swiveling left and right. No sounds. No movement. "I think we did it."

Griffin hurried into the house and returned with the cake package. "Maybe we have some luck after all."

He ran past the next house with Jen behind him, stopped and scouted the road, then continued to the other house. Jen caught up and grabbed his arm. "My dad."

"Where was he when you last saw him?"

She tried to get her bearings. The house they stood next to looked the same as any other, battered by the elements, with a four-wheeler outside and a snow machine with a tarp draped over half of it.

"It was either right where we're standing, or that next house closer to the school."

"I'll search the next house. You check out this one." Griffin peered beneath the house. "Nothing under there. Be quick." He ran across the road.

Jen climbed the stairs, her stomach dropping when she hit a squeaky step. She paused, then proceeded when nothing happened.

The door was closed and blankets hung on the inside of the windows. She turned the knob and eased the door open. Gripping the bat like her life depended on it, she stepped inside and closed the door, then fumbled on the wall for the light switch.

She flipped a switch. Dull light cast shadows over a tidy, but threadbare room. Family pictures hung on the wall alongside various skins and animal trophies. An ivory dream catcher hung from the ceiling in the center.

"Dad," Jen said.

Two doors stood at the back of the house. She pressed her ear against one. "Dad, are you there?"

Nothing stirred. She pushed the door open and flipped the light on. A lumpy bed on a rusted metal frame lay against a wall. A new-looking handmade blanket lay on it.

Jen opened the other room and lit it. Two single beds, a few toys, and children's clothes scattered about.

Shit. "Dad? Chris?"

Maybe they'd returned to the school. *I swear I'm not leaving this village without them.*

She left the house and stood on the porch, scanning for any sign of trouble. Griffin stood across the road. He held his hands up and shook his head.

Where the hell are they?

She walked toward Griffin, but stopped. A noise. *A rustle.*

The tarp on the snow machine moved in the wind. She let out a long breath. *Getting jumpy.*

But the tarp moved again, near the bottom. "That's not the wind."

She raised the bat over her head and stalked toward the tarp. It rustled again, but without a gust of wind blowing first. Something pressed against the inside of the tarp. *Not an animal. Too big.*

Swallowing, Jen leaned forward and grasped the end of the tarp with one hand. She glanced at Griffin, who hurried to join her.

She yanked the tarp off, and on the ground staring at her was Marcia's father. He tilted his head back and let out a blood curdling shriek.

26

Jen brought the bat down on the old man's skull, silencing him in mid-screech. Griffin ran up. "Marcia's father?"

Shaking the blood off the bat, Jen said, "Yeah. He takes a licking, but keeps on ticking."

Several answering shrieks sounded from the direction of the M80 detonations. Griffin didn't need to tell her what to do. Jen raced toward the school. She beat Griffin there by seconds and pulled the door open.

"Where are you going?" he asked.

"My dad might be in here."

Griffin pointed back the way they'd come. "I don't think so."

Devin and Chris trotted toward them. Jen ran to her dad and clutched him to her. "I thought you were gone."

"Can't get rid of me that easy," he murmured.

She released him. "Where the hell were you?"

"We saw we weren't going to make it and didn't want you two coming back to get us, so we hid behind the house until the horde passed."

Chris nodded at the school. "Then we came back here until we heard the fireworks."

Griffin took the cake out of the package and laid it on the ground twenty feet from the school's entrance. "Get over here. I need to light this before the drizzle screws it up."

Jen pulled Devin over with her. When they reached Griffin, Devin bent over with his hands on his knees. Jen put a hand on his back. "You OK?"

"Just out of shape," he gasped. "I'm good to go."

"You're going to have to be," Griffin said. "We can't wait any longer."

Chris walked over, his eyes scanning the area. "Why don't the rest of us wait for Griffin on the other side of the school?"

Devin straightened. Jen took his hand and they followed Chris. By the time they reached the other entrance, Devin's breathing had slowed and become less raspy. Even his color seemed better.

Griffin streaked toward them, waving for them to get moving. The group raced from the school as a boom came from behind and the sky lit up in blues and greens. Another blast, then dozens of smaller explosions followed, as if a hundred firecrackers went off in the sky.

Zombie screeches rose but were drowned out by the fireworks.

Griffin zigzagged between buildings and almost ran into a sailor as he rounded a corner. The zombie let out a quick screech, but Jen's bat dropped the creature. No answering shrieks came.

They passed Raymond's house as the big finale—a cascading rainbow of colors with big explosions punctuating the show—burst over the village. Jen broke onto the road and headed for the community center. "Didn't think I'd be glad to see this place again."

Devin stumbled in and slumped onto a chair, his lungs heaving. Jen found water and brought him some. "You take it easy," she said. He nodded, unable to speak.

Pools of drying blood lay on the floor, especially near the doors. Half-eaten organs were strewn everywhere, clouds of flies buzzing above them. Jen checked the doorways for weapons, but found nothing more than pieces of wood suitable for clubs.

"Jen." Griffin stood in the kitchen area holding a revolver.

She hurried over and took it from him. Popping the cylinder open, she checked the rounds. "Only two left unfired."

Chris stood at the back door, looking out. He turned to the others. "The villagers are already coming back."

"Shit." Jen closed the cylinder and stuck the revolver in her belt. "We better get up that freaking hill."

They left the community center single file out the front door, with Chris taking them in a wide arc to the base of the hill. He looked at his watch. "The plane should've been here twenty minutes ago."

"Then we should get to the boats," Devin said. "We can't stick around here any longer."

Chris looked up the hill. "Stay on the far edge. The middle is all mud." He clambered up the slope and didn't look back. Griffin followed.

Jen turned to Devin. "You first. I'll hold the rear."

"I'm supposed to protect you," Devin said.

Jen took his hand. "We're supposed to protect each other, and this climb'll take a lot out of you." She squeezed his hand. "My turn to take care of you."

Devin kissed her on the cheek. "I bought a condo in Anchorage before we flew out here."

Jen gave him a slight push on the back. "Come on, then, old man. Let's go home."

Devin trudged up the hill and Jen kept pace behind him, maintaining watch on the houses at their rear. A few minutes later, they climbed high enough to see over the roofs. Zombies gathered in clusters, wandering aimlessly about. Jen's heart raced as she and Devin worked their way higher and she had view of the whole village. Hundreds of zombies filled the streets. *Rush hour in Zombietown.*

Devin reached the lip of the flat section of the slope and stepped onto it with one foot, but lost his balance with the other. With a cry of surprise, he slid backward. Jen caught him from sliding farther. Chris and Griffin each grasped a hand and pulled him up.

A screech sounded behind Jen. A sailor outside the community center had seen them. The call was repeated across the village, and hundreds of zombies raced for the slope.

Jen pushed her father forward. "Get out of sight. Head for the trailers."

Chris sprinted for the trailers, but skidded to a halt.

A sailor lumbered into view, and Jen took a practice swing with her bat. "This is going to be almost too easy."

The sailor shambled toward her, but Jen caught her breath as another figure rushed them, its eyes burning into hers.

Raymond.

27

Raymond screeched. He zipped past the sailor and bore down on Jen. Chris took a swipe at him, but Raymond bowled him over and continued rumbling toward Jen.

Devin jumped in front of her and slammed the pipe into Raymond's chest. It might as well have been a pillow as much as it did to slow the huge zombie. Raymond knocked Devin to the side.

Jen ducked and cracked her bat across Raymond's shin. Raymond hit the ground and tumbled over the edge of the hill. Jen ran to the edge and watched him tumble all the way to the bottom.

Griffin put a round in the sailor's forehead, and it fell in a heap.

Jen joined the others, her pulse pounding in her ears. "Son of a bitch. Raymond's damn near unstoppable."

Chris leaned on his axe and wiped the sweat from his brow. "There are too many of them. We won't make it to the boats with all the undead flooding the streets, so what do we do now? Make a last stand in the trailers?"

"They won't hold," Devin said. "Too flimsy. Our only choice is to go up to the landing strip."

Snarls sounded closer from three sides. Griffin looked down the slope. "Most of them can't make it up through the mud. They keep slipping back down, but there's still a couple dozen or more on their way up the sides."

"What then?" Chris picked his axe up.

Jen's gaze fell on the fuel tank a hundred feet up the hill. "We burn them?"

Griffin jogged back to her. "What?"

"Chris can punch a hole in the side of the fuel tank with the axe. It empties down the hill and into the village, and we light it. Might not take them all out, but it could kill enough of them to give us a fighting chance to make it to the boats."

Chris smiled. "Brilliant." He ran around the trailer and toward the tank.

Jen pulled Devin's arm. "Let's go, Dad."

The first wave of zombies reached the trailer just as she arrived at the tank. One of the creatures spotted them and let out a screech that was echoed by the rest.

Chris reached in his pocket and tossed something to Jen. She caught it. It was the Marine Corps lighter. Leo's lighter.

He hefted the axe. "Be ready to light the fuel when I tell you, but you'd better stand back. You don't want to get any of it on you."

Griffin grabbed her wrist. "No. That tank'll explode. We have to be under cover first."

Shit. Jen looked around, her gaze falling on the trailers. Running downhill, they could reach them in seconds. And the fuel would flow right by. She pointed at the trailers. "We'll all take cover behind them."

Chris nodded. Jen joined Devin and Griffin a few yards to the side. She pulled the revolver from her belt, while Griffin's face hardened and he faced the incoming zombies with his .357. "Six rounds left," he said.

Devin's eyebrows lowered on his ashen face. "Make them count."

Chris grunted and attacked the tank with the axe. It bounced off the side, leaving a small dent. He reared back and swung again. The dent didn't seem to get deeper.

A teenage boy with a gaping chest wound reached them and Devin knocked him away with the pipe. The zombie regained its footing in seconds and rushed him. Jen aimed. *Got to time this right.* She led the zombie and squeezed the trigger. The gun clicked empty.

"Shit! I didn't line up the right fucking chamber."

The .357 Magnum boomed behind her and the teen's face imploded, spewing gore in an arc behind him.

Two more zombies reached them and Devin managed to jump out of a middle-aged man's way at the last second and whack it with the pipe. He missed the head and instead hit the back of its neck, adding a cracking sound to Chris's grunts as he swung the axe.

Griffin planted his tomahawk into the forehead of the other zombie and stepped in front of Devin as the middle-aged man counter-attacked. He didn't have time to recover from his last strike, but managed to push the zombie to the ground.

Jen turned to Chris. He hadn't made any headway. "Turn it around. Hit it with the pointy end."

Chris looked at the axe head and groaned. "Of course." He reared back and drove the point into the tank. Fuel trickled out of a small hole.

"That's it," Jen yelled.

Chris punctured the tank again, and the trickle became

a stream. "Not enough. I've got to get it emptying faster than that."

Griffin shot the middle-aged zombie, then glanced down the slope. "Better hurry."

The second wave of zombies was nearly on them. Griffin lined up his sights on the horde climbing the slope and took a lead zombie down. Jen pulled her gun, popped the revolver's cylinder open, and lined up the chamber with the first live round. Griffin's gun boomed again.

Devin struggled to fight off a man with a bloody stump for an ear. He stumbled backward and fell. Jen shot the top of the zombie's skull off.

Chris widened the hole in the tank, and fuel gushed out. He backed up. "Let's take cover." A growl from behind got Jen's attention, and Raymond raced in and tackled Chris to the ground. Fuel splashed over them as Chris struggled to get him off. He managed to get up on one knee and keep Raymond's clacking jaws back, but he coughed and sputtered as the fuel poured over him.

Jen lined up her sights on Raymond's head, but he moved just as she fired, and the round went through his shoulder. *Shit. Out of ammo.* She dropped the gun and picked up her bat.

Chris pushed Raymond back and struggled to his feet, but two more zombies attacked.

"Get out of there," Jen yelled.

Chris put one zombie in a headlock, but the other jumped on his back and bit into his shoulder. Chris screamed. He grabbed at the zombie on his back and ducked, flipping it over. It landed on its back a couple of feet from Jen.

Raymond grabbed Chris from behind. A dozen more zombies closed in on him, only a few yards away.

"Get down there and light it," Chris yelled.

Jen's head spun. Lighting the fuel would kill Chris. *But I have no choice. He's been bitten.*

Raymond jumped on Chris's back, bent his head down, and tore his ear off. Chris reached around, but was unable to grasp him. He screamed and flailed at the zombie.

Devin threw off another attacker and caved in its head with the pipe. He turned and faced thirty more zombies slipping on the fuel, but nearly up the slope. "Let's go."

Raymond grabbed Chris's head and turned it toward him. Chris pushed against him, but the zombie drew his face toward its mouth. Jen couldn't see what he did, but it looked like Raymond was kissing Chris on his upper cheek. Chris shrieked and Raymond released him, chewing.

Chris turned toward Jen, his empty eye socket oozing gore. "Please, Jen!"

Jen glanced at Raymond as he slurped the last of Chris's optic nerve into his mouth like a strand of spaghetti. Griffin's gun barked, and a hole appeared where Raymond's nose had been. He wobbled, then dropped.

Two more zombies piled onto Chris. He wailed as they tore into his flesh. "Jeeennnn!"

Tears streaming down her face, she grabbed her father's arm. "We need to get under cover."

Her father caved in the face of a bearded zombie. "They're between us and the trailers."

Most of the zombies had peeled off toward Chris, but nine still raced toward them. "We run through them. Knock 'em over. Like bowling pins."

Griffin charged down the hill, waving his tomahawk over his head and screaming. Jen pulled her father behind her and darted down the hill after him.

Griffin swung, and his tomahawk embedded in the lead

zombie's temple. It fell, and his weapon went with it. He rammed into another zombie, and it held onto him as they both rolled to the ground.

Jen aimed for a spot between a man with his neck torn open and a girl with an arm that looked like hamburger. Two steps before they collided, she lowered her shoulder and yelled.

She propelled the two zombies to the side, but another one was just behind them. She hit it full force, its open gut spraying her with blood and bits of innards. She stumbled, but her father pulled her along and behind the science lab trailer.

She wiped the gore from her eyes. The fuel had made it several yards past the trailers, but had pooled. "It's not going to the village," her father said. "It's seeping into the ground."

Griffin pushed himself to his knees, but three zombies piled on him. Griffin bellowed as they stripped the flesh from his arms and neck.

Jen's hands trembled as she struck the lighter's wheel. Sparks flew, but the wick didn't light.

She pressed her thumb against the wheel again. "Please light," she whimpered, and spun the wheel.

A yellow-blue flame appeared on the wick. Jen tossed it at the fuel trail, and it ignited with a *whomp*. A wall of heat drove her back and seared her skin.

Seconds later the world shook, throwing Jen and her father to the ground. The trailer tipped towards them, its roof peeling off and flying down the hill. She covered her head with her arms. The trailer wobbled, threatening to crush them, then slammed back down in an upright position. Its windows shattered and sprayed shards of glass on her and her dad.

Jen removed her arms from her face and brushed off

glass. She watched a huge fireball rise in the sky, carrying glowing embers and pieces of debris with it.

Devin picked Jen up under the arms. "We need to get to the boat. This whole village is going up."

Pieces of the flaming debris rained down, sparking fires all over the village.

Jen hugged her father. "Chris." She sobbed. "Even Griffin came through in the end."

He patted her back. "I know. But you did them a kindness. I would rather someone kill me than live as a monster. Would you do that for me if the time came?"

Numbness flooded Jen's mind. Kill her own father? She peered into his eyes and saw nothing but sincerity. *We're OK and we're getting out of here, so what does it matter?* "I will," she murmured. "I promise."

They held each other for a minute, then Jen let go and wiped her eyes. "Which way?"

Devin pointed off to the left. "I don't see anything over there."

She nodded and climbed to the top of the hill, the crackling and popping from the fires echoing in her ears. The sweet stench of burnt flesh hung in the air.

She glanced back to make sure her dad was still with her. Only a few steps behind, he held his left arm close to his body.

"What happened? Did you get bit?"

He put his good hand on her shoulder. "Just a sprain. I'm a little old to be playing zombie slayer."

She put an arm around him. "Could be a second career."

He shook his head. "Let's hope not."

28

An hour out of Point Wallace, Jen looked back. The smoke column coming from the village looked tiny. The weather had cleared, but the sea remained choppy. Devin guided the eighteen-foot boat south and kept it about a hundred yards offshore.

Soaked from the waves crashing over the gunwale, Jen shivered and hugged herself. The hot weather did little to warm her when she was splashed with frigid sea water every thirty seconds.

Devin slumped and almost fell off the bench. Jen put an arm around his shoulder and steadied him.

"You OK?"

"Not feeling well."

She put a hand over his. "Why don't you lie down? I'll take the wheel."

"Keep it on course," he said, slurring his words.

She eased him to the floor. "I think I can handle the navigation. Not exactly rocket science."

He rolled into the fetal position.

She slid behind the wheel and kept it steady. Her mind

raced. *How long will it take to get to Wainwright? Do we have enough gas? How the hell will we explain what happened?*

A whole village had gone up in smoke. People were going to demand answers, and she didn't want to give the ones they had.

A speck appeared in the sky ahead. It slowly grew larger. Her heart leapt. She recognized the sound, even from a distance. One of her ex-boyfriends had been an Army helicopter pilot and had taken her up in a civilian rental several times.

The helicopter flew toward them, following the coast. The *whup, whup* of its blades grew louder. Jen waved and whooped. "Over here. Please."

The helicopter veered from the coast and approached them, its military markings becoming clearer. A loudspeaker turned on with a squelch and a nasal voice said, "This is the Alaska National Guard. We're here to assist anyone from Point Wallace. Head to shore and we'll pick you up."

Thank God!

Jen steered the boat to a rocky beach and ran it aground. The helicopter landed fifty yards away and two soldiers jumped out.

As she helped her dad out of the boat, he slumped, his full weight on her. It took everything she had to keep from dropping him.

The soldiers were almost upon them. "We're rescued, Dad. We made it."

The men stopped short. "Are you OK, ma'am?"

"Yes. We're so glad to see you."

The other soldier pointed at her dad. "What about him?"

She smiled. "My dad. He's not feeling well. Been through a lot."

The soldiers looked at each other. Something passed between them.

"If we help him," the first soldier said, "can you make it to the chopper on your own?"

Jen nodded. "But I need to help my dad."

"We've got him. Go on." The soldiers moved in and each draped one of her father's arms over their shoulders. "Go ahead. We'll catch up."

Jen let go of her dad, and the men walked him toward the helicopter, his feet dragging on the ground. She ran ahead, remembering to duck as she approached the spinning blades.

A soldier with a visored helmet waved her forward. He pointed to a canvas-covered bench. "Sit there. Put on your harness."

She climbed in and he helped her with the straps. The other two soldiers walked her father up, and the three soldiers lifted him in and strapped him onto the bench across from her. His head still slumped forward. The soldier with the helmet examined him.

"Is he OK?" she asked.

He nodded and sidled over to her as the chopper lifted off. "How are you doing?"

"Tired. Worn out."

He reached into a bag and pulled out a syringe and a medicine vial. He stuck the needle in the bottle and drew out slightly yellow liquid into the syringe.

Uneasiness crept into her gut. "What's that?"

The soldier smiled. "Just something to relax you."

"I don't need it. I'm OK now that we're getting out of here."

He nodded at the other soldiers, and they held her down. She struggled. "I don't want it," she screamed. "Stop!"

There was a sting in her upper arm, then coldness seeped into her veins. The soldier who'd injected her checked her pulse. She already felt droopy.

He patted her shoulder. "You'll be asleep in another minute or so."

She wanted to tell him "no," but she couldn't get her mouth to work.

Her father's hands clenched and unclenched.

Jen's eyelids grew heavy. Just before she lost consciousness, her father straightened, raised his head, and opened his eyes.

His yellow eyes.

BUT WAIT, THERE'S MORE

The uprising continues in The Gauntlet, Book Two in the Zombie Uprising series. Get it now and continue the adventure at www.hyperurl.co/TheGauntletNovel

Get a free eBook and receive news and updates of coming releases, get recommendations, and enter giveaways at uprising.marobbins.com

AUTHOR'S NOTES

When I first decided to write post-apocalyptic fiction, I thought I'd start with a zombie story, since that was my favorite to read.

But when I looked at the number of zombie books available, I thought the genre was crowded and my series would get lost in the glut. So I wrote The Tilt which is a non-zombie post-apocalyptic story.

The Tilt was a great story to explore and write, and I'll finish the series in the future, but I found there are still a lot of readers out there like me—readers who read a lot of zombie fiction and still want more.

The result is the story you have just read. And there's much more coming as the zombie apocalypse strengthens and spreads. You can expect a lot of action, unique new characters, both ally and foe, and plenty of twists and turns.

Thanks for reading this book, and I hope you join me in this journey through the Zombie Uprising.

M.A.

ACKNOWLEDGMENTS

First, I want to thank my wife, Debbie, who puts up with me disappearing into my office for hours at a time. I also always appreciate my critique partners Brooke Hartman, Louise Goulet, Molly Gray, and Tam Linsey.

This book had a great group of beta readers. Thanks for making the book better: A.M. Ireland, Ellen Engelbrecht, Helen Zawacki, Katie Lee Cook, Leland Lydecker, Maureen R. Meyer, Natalie, Pete Bevan, Rachel Wagner, Shauna Joesten, 'The real Petrovich', Vinnyz, and Wayne Tripp.

My editor, Tamara Blain of A Closer Look Editing, did her usual bang-up job. I'm always amazed at the things she picks up that I missed. Domi of Inspired Cover Designs did a tremendous job on the eye-catching cover.

Mostly, I'd like to thank you, my readers. I ultimately write these books for you because I am one of you. Every email, review, and rating I get from readers is fuel for writing more books. I don't take you for granted. You're an important part of this process.

ALSO BY M.A. ROBBINS

The Zombie Uprising Series
    The Gauntlet, Book Two
    The Citadel, Book Three

The Tilt Series
    The Tilt, Book One

Printed in Great Britain
by Amazon